Samantha looked over the devastation in the kitchen. "I've ruined their house."

"Not ruined," Bret rebuked her. "Damaged. But it can be fixed."

Helplessly she stared at him.

Bret's gut told him to get as far away as possible from the one woman he'd never been able to stop loving. He'd learned to live without her, but he had never felt the same way about anyone else. Yet the deep blue of her eyes chased away his good sense. "I know my way around a saw and hammer. And I can recruit some help."

"But you have—"

Bret resisted the pull of old, unresolved feelings. He doubted he'd survive another desertion. And once she was well, he knew she would be gone again. "A friend who needs help."

Samantha's eyes, devoid of hope, flickered just a bit.

Friend… He had to keep it that way. Or he might not get over the pain this time.

Books by Bonnie K. Winn

Love Inspired

*A Family All Her Own
*Family Ties
*Promise of Grace
*Protected Hearts
*Child of Mine
*To Love Again
*Lone Star Blessings
*Return to Rosewood

*Rosewood, Texas

BONNIE K. WINN

is a hopeless romantic who has written incessantly since the third grade. So it seemed only natural that she turned to romance writing. A seasoned author of historical and contemporary romance, Bonnie has won numerous awards for her bestselling books. *Affaire de Coeur* chose her as one of the Top Ten Romance Writers in America.

Bonnie loves writing contemporary romance because she can set her stories in the modern cities close to her heart and explore the endlessly fascinating strengths of today's women.

Living in the foothills of the Rockies gives her plenty of inspiration and a touch of whimsy, as well. She shares her life with her husband, son and a spunky Norwich terrier who lends his characteristics to many pets in her stories. Bonnie's keeping mum about anyone else's characteristics she may have borrowed.

Return to Rosewood
Bonnie K. Winn

Steeple
Hill®

Published by Steeple Hill Books™

STEEPLE HILL BOOKS

Steeple
Hill®

Recycling programs
for this product may
not exist in your area.

ISBN-13: 978-0-373-81480-0

RETURN TO ROSEWOOD

www.SteepleHill.com

Printed in U.S.A.

We are troubled on every side, yet not distressed; we are perplexed, but not in despair. Persecuted, but not forsaken; cast down, but not destroyed.

—*II Corinthians* 4: 8-9

For my love, Howard.
Always and forever.

Chapter One

Ice! The ocean-sized sheet sucked her in, paralyzing, drowning her. Samantha shot up from her nightmare, drenched in sweat. Breathing so hard the gasps hurt her chest, she painfully lifted one leg, then the other over the side of the bed. She reached for her wheelchair. Still not accustomed to her damaged body, Samantha tried three times before she levered herself up from the bed.

Trembling, she wheeled slowly through her parents' home to the kitchen, which was in the rear quarter of the old, large Victorian house. Accustomed to her streamlined New York apartment, she'd forgotten how many doodads her mother had everywhere. Between the little tea tables, plants and trinkets, it was hard to navigate the distance, especially in the aftermath of her nightmare.

Hands shaking, Samantha decided to have a cup of tea. She turned the knob on the stove, but it didn't light. Ignitor switches were getting old, her mother had said months before. Samantha was lucky they'd decided to leave the utilities on in the empty house.

Muttering to herself, she searched through the lower shelves of the pantry and three drawers before she found a kitchen match. She returned to the stove. Hands not yet under control, it took her several tries to light the match.

Whoosh! Boom! With the knob set on high, gas had built up, causing it to explode.

Samantha rolled backward as the blast billowed out. Flames touched the crowded row of potholders on the cabinet directly beside the stove, then climbed to the curtain framing the large window. Silly, frilly doodads hanging on the adjoining wall erupted into flames. The heat grew, suddenly popping out the glass in the window. Air rushed in, feeding the fire.

Smoke alarms started shrieking, first in the kitchen, then in the hall as the smoke traveled. Trying not to panic, Samantha wheeled over to the small fire extinguisher that hung on the wall. She reached with all her might, but she couldn't get a decent hold on the metal cannister. Frustrated, she tried to stand, but her leg muscles were ineffectual.

Panting from exertion, she slumped back in the chair. Tempted to give into her fate, Samantha waited a few precious seconds before she pivoted and wheeled into the living room, where she'd stowed her purse. Grabbing her cell phone, she dialed 911. She didn't particularly care what happened to her, but she wasn't going to destroy her parents' house.

Fearfully watching fire eat through dry, native pine cabinets in the kitchen, Samantha gave the emergency operator the address. The house was more than a hundred years old, perfect kindling.

Samantha closed her eyes briefly, imagining the disappointment on her parents' faces. Retired teachers, they'd gone to a remote country in Africa to run a school. But the house was her mother's pride and joy, having been in her family for generations.

Coughing from the smoke, Samantha unlocked the front door for the firemen. She tried to reach the rear door in the kitchen, but the heat of the fire pressed her back.

The smoke made its way into the living room and more alarms shrieked. Her coughing intensified. She tried covering her mouth with her hands, but it didn't do much good.

A siren split the air as the fire engine screeched to a stop in front of the house. The door burst open and volunteer firemen rushed inside. She pointed toward the hall. "It's in the kitchen, in the back of the house," she gulped out between coughs.

"Anywhere else?" one man asked.

"No…." She continued coughing, then managed to speak. "At least I don't think so."

Another man grasped the handles of her wheelchair, pushing her toward the porch as soon as the last fireman cleared the doorway. He had to lift the chair over the threshold. Outside in the fresh air, Samantha continued coughing. In between, she took deep breaths to clear her lungs.

Long hoses were uncoiled, then hooked up to the fire hydrant three houses down. Some of the men carried dispensers of foam fire retardant as well. Neighbors opened their doors and windows to see what was going on.

A paramedic rushed to her side, checking for injuries.

Samantha touched her hot cheeks. "I'm not hurt. Just scorched a little of my hair."

The paramedic scanned her beneath the illumination of his flashlight, then reached for an oxygen mask. "Just want to be sure."

She brushed back the singed ends of her bangs. "I'm fine."

"You really need to get a threshold ramp in case you have to get out alone. It's an easy adaptation." The tall, muscular fireman who had wheeled her outside pulled off his mask and frowned, critically studying the front of the house. "You don't have a porch ramp either."

"Bret?" Samantha stared at the handsome man. They'd known each other since high school. And had loved each other enough to become engaged. The pain of their breakup had kept them apart for the last eight years.

He stared back, clearly startled when he recognized her.

"It's been…what?" Samantha swallowed the unexpected rush of emotions. "Since graduation?" Their days at Texas A&M seemed a lifetime ago. Strange the pain didn't.

Bret pushed back his helmet, revealing dark hair. His equally dark eyes hardened and she wondered if he was feeling the same rush of memories, the unexpected flare of attraction. *"Samantha Shaw.* Didn't expect it to be you. Thought your parents must have rented out the place." He glanced down at the chair. "Accident?"

"Yeah." It was still hard to talk about, impossible to accept.

His surprise didn't fade. "So, what are you doing in Rosewood?"

"Can't a person come home for awhile?"

"You haven't been real big on doing that."

She craned her neck, looking back at the house, trying not to think about the shock of seeing Bret.

The paramedic placed the oxygen mask over her face.

When she could speak, Samantha looked again at Bret. "Do you think there'll be much damage?"

"If it's confined to the kitchen, probably not." Bret's voice was as hard as his eyes. "Once it's clear, you can go inside for a quick look."

Her relief disappeared. "More than a quick look. I'm living here now."

"Can't do that, Sam. Not tonight. Could be a live ember left we didn't catch. It's too dangerous. You have to wait 'til it's completely cold."

Overpowered by the now familiar sense of claustrophobia and panic, she could barely speak. Not that it mattered. Surrounding neighbors who had poured out of their houses, dressed in pajamas and robes, crowded around, offering sympathy and help.

"I appreciate your concern, but it looks worse than it is." Polite but firm, Samantha declined their offers, knowing she couldn't let them in on her secret or her life.

Albert and Ethel Carruthers, the older couple who lived next door, were slow but determined as they closed in.

"Samantha!" Mrs. Carruthers clucked in worry, unfolding a crocheted afghan she'd carried with her, then smoothing it over Sam's lap. "Whatever happened?"

They were two of the very few people in Rosewood who knew she was home. Because her parents had entrusted them to watch over the house, Samantha had been forced to tell the Carratherses that she was back, especially since she'd needed their help to get inside. "Just a tiny grease fire." She tried to ignore Bret's startled expression, certain he was wondering why she was covering up the truth. "Nothing to worry about."

"But Samantha can't go back in tonight," Bret told them. He disregarded the warning in her eyes, instead talking directly to the older couple. "Could she stay at your place? Don't want her toasted by a flare-up."

"Well, of course she can!" Ethel Carruthers patted Samantha's shoulder. "It's difficult enough to be on your own, but when there's a catastrophe—"

"I wouldn't call it that," Samantha interrupted.

"Even so. What are neighbors for?"

Possibly to squeal on me. If my parents find out…

"I'll be back in a few minutes," Bret was saying. "Want to see how much damage there is."

As he walked away, Albert Carruthers stared after him, then back at Samantha. "I thought it was just a small fire."

Emotionally, Samantha felt as though she'd just run a hundred miles. The irony made her even wearier. She hated fibbing to these people—she'd known them literally her entire life. "You know how firemen are extra cautious. I don't see why I can't stay here tonight."

"Don't even think about it." Ethel had moved on to her mother-hen mode. "We keep the guest room set up all the time. Never know when one of the grands or great-grands will stop over."

Samantha softened at the longing in the older woman's voice. Her grandchildren were grown and Ethel missed them.

"Maybe we should call your parents," Ethel mused.

"No!"

Ethel's eyes widened and Samantha tried to control her flustered response. "Why worry them? It's a tiny fire. They gave up so much time flying to New York when…when I had my accident. It'd be just like them to hop on an airplane and come home."

"Well…"

"Going to Africa's been their dream since…well, *before* they retired. The kids in their school need them more than I do right now. We agreed we wouldn't ruin that for them."

Ethel sighed. "You've always been determined.

Ever since you were a little thing. You could barely toddle, but you were relentless."

Swallowing, Samantha tried not to think of those days, a time when she believed anything was possible. "My days of toddling are in the past."

Bret came up behind them. "I'm going to open the windows, let the house air out tonight. That'll help the kitchen cool down sooner, too."

Samantha squeezed her eyes shut for a brief moment, not wanting her emotions to spill over in front of him. But the lack of control, the inability to do things on her own anymore…. The pain was so intense she felt it pierce her chest. Instinctively, she pulled off the oxygen mask.

"I can come back in the morning for a few minutes before work," Bret continued. "Check out the house and take you back." He turned off the oxygen tank and placed the mask on top of it.

Not allowing Samantha to agree or refuse, he again took charge of her chair, wheeling her toward the house next door. Logically, she knew the elderly Carruthers would have a difficult time coping with her chair, but she hated when others simply took over as though her mind didn't work any better than her legs.

The Carrutherses trailed a good distance behind. Bret chose the back door of their house, tipping and then lifting Samantha's chair over the threshold in two efficient moves. "I'll wait till tomorrow to ask why you're back." He pushed the chair through the kitchen and into the living room. "And why you lied."

Startled, she stared up at him. Hearing the Carrutherses entering the house, Samantha didn't try to explain. But she knew the reprieve wouldn't last past the night.

The morning air still held the bitter aroma of charred wood. Inside Samantha's house, though, the fire was completely banked, no live embers hiding beneath the wreckage.

Bret Conway knew Samantha so well it was clear she was hiding something. Even though he shouldn't be, he was bothered by the defeat he'd glimpsed in her eyes. There'd never been an ounce of defeat in Samantha Shaw.

Just the opposite. She had been set on becoming a botanist and discovering new species. She'd traveled the globe, searching out varieties never before cataloged. Universities lined up, requesting her lectures. And as a plant pathologist, she was in constant demand. Even though Bret had gone after the same degree in school, he'd never had the same aspirations. There were wanderers and there were stayers. Samantha was a wanderer. But he needed his roots in Rosewood, to stay connected to what mattered.

So he'd used his horticulture degree to specialize in native species, in efforts to make them thrive again, to help his own corner of the planet. Or at least his corner of Texas.

And he'd known that when Samantha left Rosewood, it was for good.

Holding the newspaper he'd picked up on the lawn, Bret knocked on the Carrutherses' front door. Hearing the slow shuffle of feet, he waited patiently.

Albert didn't bother to check who was standing on the porch, pulling open the door as soon as he reached it. "That you, Bret?"

"Yes, sir. How're you doing this morning?" He held out the paper.

"Same as every other day." Albert accepted the newspaper, but didn't glance at it. The biggest local news would be the fire next door. "Come have some coffee."

Bret followed the older man into the kitchen. Ethel stood at the stove and Samantha was at the table. "Smells good."

"If that means you want a waffle, pull up a chair," Ethel replied. "I don't guess young men cook for themselves."

Amused, at the age of thirty, to be included in the young people category, he sat down across from Samantha. "If you don't plan to stay here, I will. Last time I had a waffle for breakfast…well, I don't know the last time I had one."

"Your mother must make them," Ethel chided.

He grinned. "I live in the apartment over the business, but I don't go to their house for breakfast."

Samantha fiddled nervously with her fork, but her plate was almost full. Looked like she'd only eaten a bite or two. The Samantha he knew ate with gusto, lived with even more. And she'd rarely been nervous.

No, she followed her own path even when it meant breaking his heart.

Bret's appetite vanished. He shoved back his chair. "Ethel, it pains me to say this, but I've already eaten. Sam, you ready to look at your place?"

Relief flooded the delicate features of Samantha's face. "Yes."

"But you've barely touched your breakfast," Ethel fussed.

"It was delicious, really." Samantha's smile was strained. "But I need to see the house."

Albert's brow furrowed, his long, gray eyebrows pulling together. "There shouldn't be much damage from a little grease fire."

"No, no. Of course not," Samantha's words tumbled out too quickly. Then she took a breath. "But you know how my mother feels about her house."

Ethel wiped her hands on a small terry towel. "Like any woman. Go on then. You probably won't get a decent meal 'til you've seen the kitchen."

Samantha wheeled back from the table. Bret stepped forward and opened the door. She tried to push herself over the threshold, but the chair stuck. He tipped it, lifting the wheels over the low barrier.

Bret waited until they were on the grass, heading away from the Carrutherses'. "I see you're still trying to push past anything that gets in your way."

Surprisingly, she didn't pop back with a quick retort.

The front door to her house was the only one open, since the back entry was a mess. He pivoted her wheelchair around so that she faced away from the house. "Hang on." Lifting the chair carefully up the steps, then over the threshold, he rolled her inside. They headed down the hall toward the kitchen.

As they got within viewing distance, Samantha gasped, hands flying to cover her mouth.

When she didn't speak, he pushed the chair slowly toward the center of the carnage. The beautiful, hand-carved pine cabinets were charred beyond recognition. The tall ceiling, once graced by stamped tin tiles, was now scorched, the tiles barely hanging on. Limestone counters had fallen into the remains of the lower cabinets after they'd collapsed.

The damage was exacerbated by the steady supply of air that had coursed through the shattered window. With the exception of the appliances and counters, the kitchen had been ideal fuel.

Despite opening all the windows the previous evening, the acrid smell still permeated the house. But Samantha wasn't coughing. Instead, her head was bent, face in hands.

"Sam?"

The unexpected sound of weeping startled him. She wasn't one to cry. When they'd broken their engagement, she'd shown regret, but even that had been tempered by the excitement of her plans. And there hadn't been a single tear.

"Sam?" He knelt down, then peeled her fingers back. "I know it looks bad, but it can be fixed up just fine."

Her crying deepened, her words gulping out between the sobs. "How am I going to pay to fix this?"

"Is that all?" Exasperated, Bret searched for a handkerchief. "The insurance company will cover it. All but the deductible."

She shook her head. "The house is supposed to be vacant. The insurance won't pay."

His frown deepened. "Just explain the situation. Your parents can—"

"No!" For the first time, her voice gained strength. "They can't know!"

He sat back on his heels. "What?"

"They don't know I'm here." Spent, the spirit in her voice drained away.

"What's going on?"

Samantha ran her fingers over the chair's handles, finally lifting a fragile hand to push her long, dark hair back. "I'm supposed to be in a rehabilitation facility in New York."

His eyes dropped to her legs.

"I was working on a project in upstate New York. We had a freak snowstorm in the middle of spring. I was on top of a roof. Didn't see the ice until it was too late. Landed a story below." Her words stumbled to a halt, but he didn't try to fill the long silence. "I was in a coma at first and in the hospital for months—spinal injury. My parents rushed back from Africa. When it was obvious I wasn't getting better, they started talking about bringing me back here—putting all their plans on hold. Or, I should say, canceling them. I convinced them to pack up my apartment, sublet it, then get me to a New York rehab."

He didn't understand. "Why can't they know you decided to come home instead?"

"I came back because I couldn't afford to stay in the rehab place."

"But insurance—"

She sniffled. "If I didn't know better, I'd think you took up selling insurance. Didn't have any."

His eyes widened.

Samantha was immediately defensive. "I was self-employed. I'm relatively young. I *was* healthy. Took all my savings to pay for the hospital."

"What did the doctors say about your leaving?"

Her lips clamped into a firm line.

"So what was your prognosis?"

"That with therapy I could improve."

Bret frowned again. "Then, why—"

"What doctor's going to tell two hopeful parents that I'm stuck in this chair for life?" The defiance faded and silent tears slipped from her eyes.

Failing to find a handkerchief, Bret leaned closer, using his thumbs to ease the teardrops from her cheeks. "Your parents would have understood."

"Exactly." Her deep blue eyes searched his. "You know everything they've been through—losing Andy." She bent her head at the mention of her deceased brother. He'd been killed in a small airplane crash five years earlier. "They finally managed to find enough sponsorship to start the school, to help kids the way he wanted to. And they're supposed to give all that up to come back and nurse me?"

"It's what parents do, Sam. Families."

"Just get hurt over and over again?" She searched his eyes. "Aren't they supposed to have dreams, too?"

Bret vividly remembered how she'd destroyed his dreams. "Family never was your first priority."

The past reared up between them. When Samantha had been ready to pursue her far-flung career, Bret couldn't leave Rosewood. His father was waiting for a heart transplant. While his mother took care of him, Bret stepped into his father's shoes at the family nursery. His younger sister was still in high school at the time.

Bret had begged Sam to stay in Rosewood. She suggested that they hire someone to run his father's business. She didn't understand that it was more than just keeping the nursery going. There hadn't been a certainty that his father would get the transplant in time. And Bret couldn't abandon his family. At an impasse, their engagement ended.

Pain flashed in Samantha's large eyes.

Although they hadn't had any contact in eight years, he'd known about Andy's death. Bret wondered now, as he had then, if the loss had brought home the importance of family.

Her wounded gaze lifted to the devastation in the kitchen. "Now I've ruined their house."

"Not ruined," he rebuked. "Damaged. But it can be fixed."

Helplessly, she stared at him.

His gut told him to run. To get as far away as possible from the one woman he'd never been able to forget. He'd learned to live without her, but he'd never felt the same way about anyone else. Yet, as they always had, the deep blue of her eyes chased away his good sense. "I can recruit some help to work on the kitchen."

"But you have—"

Bret resisted the pull of old, unresolved feelings. He doubted he'd survive another desertion. And once she was well, he knew she'd be gone again. "A friend who needs help."

Samantha's eyes, devoid of hope, flickered just a bit.

Friend… He had to keep it that way. Or he might not get over the pain this time.

Chapter Two

Birdsong floated through the open bedroom window, the curtain stirring in the morning breeze. Still unaccustomed to the small-town sounds of her youth, Samantha yawned. Arms stretched out elbow to elbow, hands rubbing still sleepy eyes, she halted at a new, unexpected sound.

Hammering. Or shooting?

Something was peppering the house. From the sound of it, nails or bullets must be hitting nearly the entire place.

Reaching toward the end of the bed, she grabbed a sweatshirt. She pulled it over her flannel pajama top and levered herself out of bed. Wheeling to the front door, she pulled it open. Still not oriented, she craned her head, looking for the source of the noise.

"Morning." Bret spoke from her right, standing off on the grass.

"What are you doing?" She tried to see, but couldn't push herself over the threshold.

"Porch ramp."

She gestured behind into the house. "You offered to help with the kitchen. Why—?"

He looked pointedly at her stuck chair. "And if there's another fire?"

"Institutionalize me."

"You can't afford it." Bret's somber face loosened for a moment and he flashed the same wide grin she remembered. He hadn't changed that much since college. Sun-streaked brown hair, year-round tan, dark eyes that had always seemed full of laughter. If he'd aged, it was only to the good. No longer a youth; all the harder edges of manhood suited him.

"I'm putting the ramp over here so when you're on your feet again, you can use the steps." He shot more nails into the wood structure.

Samantha wasn't a quitter, but she'd heard enough of the doctors talking when they consulted to know what her chances were. Amazing how candid they were when under the assumption the patient was asleep. It'd been the only way to find out anything. Asking questions hadn't gotten her anywhere.

Bret jumped up on the side of the porch, his tall, muscled form scaling it easily. Before she guessed his intent, he grasped her arm rests, then pushed the chair back. "I ordered a threshold adapter—two, actually. Until we get your kitchen fixed, you'd better plan on breakfast at the café. Why don't you get ready while I finish up?"

Shaking her head, Samantha grabbed the wheels and rolled backward. "No!"

Puzzled, he frowned. "What?"

"And announce to the entire town that I'm here?"

"How long do you think you can hide?" He gestured toward the houses flanking hers. "You've got relatives and friends in Rosewood. You plan on never leaving the house? Never answering the door? Or the phone?"

"My parents put the phone on suspend." It was a weak defense, but the only one she had.

Bret tapped a booted foot on the porch.

"Okay. So I didn't completely think the plan out." Samantha glanced down at her lifeless legs. "But I'll figure out something."

"You'd have a better chance of folks not spilling your secret if you tell them first. People around here don't appreciate being lied to."

She swallowed. "I do know how Rosewood works."

His eyes darkened further. "You sure about that?"

Between them, he'd always been the logical one, the most grounded. Certainly the one most connected to Rosewood. "Looks like you think I don't have any claim to my hometown."

"How long have you been here?"

"Few days." It had been an excruciating trip, managing first the plane and then the bus ride on her own. She couldn't even handle the small suitcase she'd brought along. Some strangers had taken pity on her, helping open doors occasionally. But she'd already wearied of pity while she was in the hospital. It wasn't any more palatable because she needed help. And she'd hated having to enlist the Carruthers to pick her up at the bus station, then struggle to get her wheelchair through the back door. They'd been disapproving, believing she should contact her parents immediately. Ridiculously, she felt on the edge of tears again.

"How are you getting groceries? Supplies?"

She shrugged. Hunger wasn't her problem. "Mrs. Carruthers keeps bringing over food. I told her not to."

"Have you eaten breakfast?"

Sam shook her head.

"I didn't think so." He glanced at his watch, then pulled his eyebrows together in an annoyed crease. "Rosewood's a hard place to keep a secret. Just having lights on in the house has probably gotten someone talking."

Weary both physically and emotionally, she felt like a wound-down clock. Overwhelmed, underequipped. Neither was her style. Now it was her fate.

A short time later, Bret pulled into the parking lot of Conway's Nursery. All the lights were off; none of the displays were set out front. Peter, his assistant manager, hadn't opened yet. And it was a good thirty minutes past opening time. Bret slid out of his Blazer and stomped across the lot.

As he singled out the building key, Bret noticed that the door didn't look firmly closed. He stepped back a few inches. The sign indicating whether they were open was flipped to *Closed*. Pushing on the door lightly, it opened. "Peter?"

Silence.

Bret glanced back at the parking lot, which was empty. Peter always drove to work. Turning on the inside lights, Bret could see that the ledger was laid out on the main counter. Peter was supposed to have closed up the previous evening, which meant locking the ledger in the small office.

Heading to the back of the shop, Bret didn't need long to see the office wasn't locked, either. A too familiar anger grew. Peter had been slacking off more and more. And it was at the worst possible time.

The recession hadn't spared Rosewood. People didn't consider plants a vital necessity. As receipts shrunk, Bret had been forced to rethink his business plan. He'd offered retirement packages to his three oldest employees. That had left him with Peter, whose redeeming quality was superior horticulture knowledge, and two young women who had agreed to share one position.

However, as each woman found a full-time job elsewhere, they'd left. And, now it was just Bret and Peter. Unfortunately, Peter had taken the changes as a permanent job guarantee.

Grabbing the phone, he punched in Peter's number. It rang and rang. Bret slammed the phone down hard enough to make the base rattle.

Just then he heard Peter's old Camaro screech into the lot, the low underside scraping on the driveway as it did every day.

Bret gritted his teeth as Peter took his time dragging into the store.

Peter paused to flip the sign on the door to *Open*.

"Turn it back."

Surprised, Peter frowned. "It's time."

"It's past time."

Shrugging, Peter yawned. "No customers."

"If anyone had come when we're supposed to be open, do you think they'd wait around until you decided to show up?"

Peter sighed, a long-suffering sound that told Bret that he wouldn't listen. Certainly wouldn't change.

"We've talked about this…I don't know. What? More than a dozen times now?" Bret raised his voice. "You're constantly late. Last night you didn't bother to put the ledger in the office. Not that it would've mattered. You didn't lock the office or the front door."

Peter stared at the floor, clearly bored.

"Consider yourself on probation."

"Probation?" Peter looked genuinely shocked, then amused. "You going to have the rest of the staff take over?"

"I'd do as well running the place by myself. At least I wouldn't lead the wolf to the hen house."

"Hen house?"

How such a dimwit could be so talented with plants mystified Bret. "Just worry about your probation. Ninety days. Clean up your act or you're out."

Anger flashed in the man's muddy-colored eyes and he pinched his lips together.

Bret waited to see if Peter would save him the trouble and quit.

Instead, Peter picked up his scruffy backpack and stalked off toward the office.

Bret remembered his promise to Sam that he'd pick up breakfast at the café. "Just a minute."

Peter slowed down, but didn't come to a complete stop.

"I'm going out for awhile. Anything comes up, you can reach me on my cell."

"Whatever."

Regretting hiring the man for the thousandth time, Bret turned the sign on the door and headed to his apartment over the shop via the outside stairwell. Employing Peter had been a favor. One of his older customers, Val Gertenstal, had convinced Bret that although Peter wasn't a *people person*, he was a genius with plants. When they'd been fully staffed, Peter's odd ways hadn't mattered, since he worked in the cultivating area. Now that he was expected to help on both sides of the business, every ugly thorn was showing. And sticking into Bret's hide.

Once inside his apartment, Bret grabbed a cooler. Neighbors would eventually deluge Sam with casseroles and anything else she needed. Just as soon as the truth came out about the extent of the fire.

Frowning, he wondered if she really had changed that much. She'd always been as honest as they came. Even though it had ripped out his heart, Sam had been truthful about why she'd left years earlier. *Their priorities hadn't meshed.* Words he would never forget.

By the time Bret got back to her house, Sam was staring out the large bay window in the living room. Always independent, she had to be chafing at all the constraints.

He moved the dining room chairs away from one side of the table so Sam would have easy access. "You'd better get over here if you don't want cold eggs."

She continued to stare out the window.

"Let me rephrase. *I* don't want cold eggs, so get a move on."

Startled, she pivoted, then stared.

"Chair isn't going to roll over here on its own." He set the Styrofoam cups of coffee on the table. "You still take sugar?"

"Uh, yeah. One." She reached slowly to move the wheels.

"Eggs are all scrambled. Thought that was easier. Della put in bacon, sausage and I don't know what all."

"Della's still at the café?"

"Yep. And still telling me to eat my vegetables."

That edged out a smile as Samantha neared the table. "Guess she thought we ought to eat something besides French fries."

"A potato *is* a vegetable." Watching, he saw her glance at the food.

The arms of Samantha's wheelchair fit easily beneath the century-old mahogany table. Although the house was Victorian, the furnishings were Edwardian and simpler in nature. They had been passed down along with the house. Samantha's mother, Joyce, had added her own touches—particularly her love of collectibles, lots of collectibles. Still, the house hadn't changed that much since it was built, aside from updates to the kitchen and bathrooms. But Bret suspected it was far different from Sam's New York style.

The waitress had sent along a stack of real plates and silverware. "Della said we can return this stuff whenever."

"So she knows?" Samantha asked in a small voice.

"Have to start somewhere. How 'bout calling your uncle later?"

Samantha ducked her head. "It would hurt his feelings if he heard from somebody else." Her father's brother, Uncle Don, and his family had always been close to hers. Joyce, an only child, didn't have as many relatives. "I've made a real mess of things, haven't I?"

"Not yet."

The self-pity faded from her eyes. "Gee, don't hold back. Say what you think."

"You already know what I think."

She sniffed the delicious aroma of fresh biscuits. "Hard to miss."

He handed her a biscuit on a small plate. "We have enough condiments to open our own café."

Her fragile hand shook as she picked up the biscuit and took a bite. Even though Sam had always been petite, she'd also been physically strong and active. It shocked him that she was so thin it looked like the breeze from a hand-held fan would blow her over. As she concentrated on her biscuit, Bret took the opportunity to scoop some eggs onto her plate.

"I'd forgotten how good these are." Sam took a second tiny bite of the warm, buttery biscuit. "Almost as good as my mom's." She glanced down at the eggs on her plate. "I can't eat all that."

"Then how do you expect to get better?"

Sam lifted her chin. "I don't."

"Yeah."

"I made my peace with it."

"Right."

She drew her eyebrows together. "Don't trip over your empathy."

"Don't intend to. You have to want to get better."

Her eyes suddenly blazed, something he remembered well. "You think I *want* to be in this chair?"

Bret reached for the bacon. "You're not doing much to get out of it."

She gulped back a deep breath. "You don't know what you're talking about."

"You never used to be a quitter. The Samantha I knew would be doing everything she could to walk again."

The blaze faded. "Yeah, well, maybe you don't know me anymore."

"So that's it? You can't afford rehab so you're just giving up?"

"What do you suggest I do? Rob a bank? Might be a little problem with the getaway."

The old Samantha was still there. She just didn't know it.

Samantha twisted her hands together as she waited nervously for her Uncle Don. He'd been shocked to hear she was back in Rosewood, but he'd also sounded excited.

Bret had stayed to work on the ramp. He had told her flatly he wasn't leaving until the ramp and a temporary threshold adjustment were finished. She'd almost forgotten how bossy he could be. Sam wished he would stay until her family came and give her a little moral support. Which was totally stupid, since he was clearly trying to leave as fast as he could. He'd been pounding in nails as if he had a tornado at his heels.

Not wanting to sit in front of the large bay window looking like a waif, she'd chosen to wait in the living room. Still, she could hear the rumble and lift of voices outside. Her uncle hadn't come alone. Nor did he make it through the door first. Her cousin and best friend, Rachel, ran inside, not stopping until she was inches away. Her hug was as unexpected as Samantha's tears. *Get a grip.*

Then she saw matching tears on Rachel's face. An overwhelming need to give in to her own assailed Sam.

"I can't believe you didn't tell us." Hoarse with emotion, Rachel ignored her own tears as she brushed Samantha's away.

There was no explanation she could offer.

Rachel's mother, Trudy, came inside, her movements stiff. With her arthritic arms outstretched, she saw Sam and her face began to crumple.

Don, the last one inside, shook his head. "What's this? A weeping convention?" A few long strides and he was next to her with a hug as well.

When the tears subsided, Samantha faced them all. "I didn't mean to exclude you. I…just hadn't thought out what it would mean coming back here."

"This is your home." Don, only two years older than her father, Ed, looked nearly enough like him to be his twin. "You never have to think out coming home. But we'd like to make things easier for you."

Although he was wise enough to hide his pity, Samantha knew it was there. "But that's just it. I don't want anyone to take care of me…to worry."

"It comes with the territory. Rachel contends she's an adult who can live her own life. I suppose she's right, but it doesn't stop us worrying. That's what family does."

The years away from Rosewood had dimmed her sense of family, what the connections really meant. But ever since her brother, Andy, had died….

Sniffling, Rachel playfully punched her dad's arm. "You'd think I was twelve years old."

"Don't believe otherwise," Trudy advised, wiping her own face. "As far as your father's concerned, you'll always be twelve."

Don glanced in the kitchen. "Looks like we've got some work to do."

"But—"

He held up one hand. "Bret filled me in before he left. I'm no carpenter, but I'll do what I can. You'll get plenty of help from your friends and neighbors."

Samantha felt she'd been gone too long to expect anything from them. But that was how Rosewood worked. People pitched in together. They might be a dying breed, but the small town's citizens believed in neighbor helping neighbor.

"I thought your dad was being extravagant when he told me he planned to keep the utilities on," Don continued. "Said a house slowly disintegrates when it's left closed up."

"He knows how much the house means to Mom."

Don nodded in agreement. "Oh, and Miss Leeson comes in to clean twice a month. You'd have given her a heart attack."

The complications were multiplying. "Uncle Don, you can't tell Mom or Dad."

He pursed his lips.

"Promise…please?"

Reluctance swamped his face, but he finally nodded. "As long as you're okay. That changes and the promise is off."

Samantha knew she was lucky he wasn't already dialing the phone. "Thanks." The emotional reunion was exhausting. Had it only been months since she could trek for hours on end hunting a new species? Traveling to South America, Asia, pushing through the rain forests and jungles as easily as walking from one room to another. Now she was exhausted from sitting and talking a few minutes.

Rachel noticed. "Mom, Dad, we're wearing Sam out."

"But we just got here!" Trudy protested.

Don took her arm. "Rachel's right. Sam, we'll leave for today, but we'll be back. Often."

Touched, again she felt the threat of tears. Not a crier, she hated the weakness. "Thanks, Uncle Don."

He clasped her shoulder. "You've got a lot to deal with, Sam. Remember you don't have to do it alone."

Not sure whether her voice would warble, she nodded.

Her Aunt Trudy looked as though she was ready to start the waterworks again, so Samantha dredged up a smile.

Rachel leaned close. "Don't worry, Sam. We'll get those legs working again. And you've got my cell number. I don't care if it's three a.m., you need something—call."

Samantha returned her cousin's hug, and kept the smile on her face until they were gone. Then she stared at her legs. She couldn't tell them. She couldn't tell anyone. There was no hope. No chance. Not unless there was a miracle. And she'd stopped believing in those the day Andy died.

Chapter Three

By late afternoon, Bret had left the nursery in Peter's less-than-capable hands. Not that he wanted to, but he needed to make his daily run to his parents' home to check on his father.

Robert's health had been delicate since his heart transplant. So much so that he'd retired when Bret graduated from Texas A&M. Over the years, Bret had transformed the old family nursery. Robert had approved of the changes, understanding the need to grow native species that didn't require watering. Not that Robert wanted to stop selling traditional bedding plants, too.

And although he couldn't work at the nursery any longer, Robert kept busy growing orchids, a process as delicate as his health.

Bret quickly walked up the weathered brick driveway, nearing the garage, which was actually an old carriage house. It went with the age of the house, which had been built around the turn of the last century. It wasn't a fancy house, but one that always said home. Welcoming, warm, comforting. Thick ivy grew up the brick exterior, framing the front door, outlining the windows, wrapping the house in a protective green layer. Each flower bed was laid out with loving care so that something bloomed most all year.

Bret passed beneath heirloom roses that climbed the arched trellis leading to the backyard. The glass greenhouse where he was headed was nearly as old as the house. His parents said it had been a deciding factor when they'd purchased the house. The Victorian greenhouse had fallen into disrepair with the previous owners, but his parents, then young and healthy, had lovingly restored the building.

The arid conditions in the Hill Country weren't a good match for Robert's exotic orchids, but the greenhouse was equipped with steam-driven humidity. Back in the early 1900s, the lady of the house no doubt had kept her most treasured plants in the large, adjacent conservatory.

Bret paused, glancing at the huge old magnolia tree that shaded the back porch. Dinner-plate-sized blossoms nestled amidst glossy, deep-green leaves, perfuming the entire yard.

Hearing his father humming, Bret stepped into the moist air of the greenhouse. "Hey, Dad."

"Bret!" Pleasure filled his father's voice. Then he looked closely at his son. "Something wrong?"

"I must be completely transparent." Bret dropped on a stool near his father.

"It's a parent thing." Robert laid down his pruning shears, then pulled off his gloves.

"Samantha's back in town."

Eyebrows lifted, Robert pursed his lips. "Been awhile."

"Yeah." Bret hooked one boot over the stool's railing.

"Something special bring her home?"

"She had a bad accident. Her legs are paralyzed."

Shocked, Robert stared at him. "Permanently?"

Bret shrugged. "She thinks so."

"Her parents must be frantic."

"They don't know she's here." He explained Sam's reasoning. "Sam knows they'll find out. She's just hoping to put it off for awhile."

Robert scrunched his brow in concentration. "I saw something in the paper about a grease fire at the Shaw home. Nothing about Sam in the article, though."

"That's because she was already in the Carruthers house by the time the kid from the paper came to take pictures. And the neighbors repeated what Sam had said about it being a small fire."

"Hmm."

"She didn't even have a ramp put in. Lucky she didn't roast herself."

Concern etched deeper lines in Robert's face. "Is she all right?"

"That's what I've been doing today, making sure… building a ramp, putting in threshold adapters."

Robert waited.

"I'm going to talk to Matt Whitaker. See if he'll

build some new cabinets—try and replicate the originals. That, and round up some more volunteers."

"Wish I were stronger. I'd help."

Despite everything his dad had endured, he still reached out to help others. He donated his prized orchids to be auctioned off for charity, supplied cut flowers to the church for Sunday services. And he never felt sorry for himself. Something Sam needed to learn. "You help, Dad. Listening." Exhaling, Bret flipped his keys.

"Something else, son?"

"Peter. Put him on probation today."

Robert frowned. He hadn't been happy that employees who had been with him since the start of the business had retired, but he'd understood. "That boy doesn't belong in a position where he deals with people."

"I know. Maybe I can find someone else. Budget's still tighter than a bale of cotton."

"I hadn't wanted to say anything, with all you've got on your plate, but Herb got laid off."

"When?"

"Last week. Your mother and sister insist on sounding positive all the time about how he'll get another job. I guess they're afraid I'll wilt under the strain."

Herb, Bret's brother-in-law, had worked for an independent oil man, heading the local office. "How are they going to manage the office without Herb?"

"They're not. Decided to close it, consolidate it with operations in East Texas."

While Rosewood was a wonderful place to live, a mecca of new jobs it wasn't. "Do you think Herb would want to work at the nursery? I know it's not as high-tech as what he's used to, but maybe it would help in the interim."

"You just said the budget's—"

"Herb's family. How are Janie and the kids going to make it without his income? It'd be a cut in salary, but more than unemployment. And, maybe, if he's around, it'll light a fire under Peter."

"A tanker full of gasoline wouldn't do that."

They both laughed.

"Or Peter might get mad enough to quit." Bret shook his head. "Of course, knowing Peter, he'll stay on just to get under my skin."

Herb and Janie's small house sat on the end of a quiet lane. His sister had the family green thumb and their yard was the prettiest on the street.

He rang the bell. The sounds of his niece and nephews running and shrieking poured out when Janie swung open the door.

"Wow. You never come at dinner time. What's up?"

Sibling shorthand made it easy for them to get straight to the point.

"Don't want to eat. Thanks anyway. Herb around?"

"He's out back." Janie frowned. "Something wrong?"

"Yep. You could have told me about his job."

Her face fell. "We didn't want to worry you."

"First Dad, now me?"

She trailed him as far as the kitchen. "Do you want to stay for dinner?"

The conciliatory gesture made him smile. Especially since Janie hated cooking.

Out back he found Herb trimming the already precisely edged shrubs lining the back fence.

"Hey."

Seeing that it was Bret, Herb smiled. "Not like you to brave the rugrats during the week."

"Actually came to see you."

Herb gestured to the padded lawn chairs surrounding a wide, planked table. "What's up?"

"Hoping you can help me out." Bret outlined Peter's behavior the last few months, ending with the disastrous morning. "So I'm wondering if you're interested in working at the nursery."

Herb's expression was knowing. "A pity job to keep me employed?"

"Nope. I know it's not ideal for you. And I'd expect you to keep on looking for something better—something like you're used to. And no problems if you find a job and have to leave without notice. But I almost fired Peter today, which would leave me with no one. I probably shouldn't have let him off with probation. I'm really hoping he'll quit."

Herb rubbed his forehead, pushing back short, light hair. "If it's really not a pity offer, I'm grateful for the work."

"Can you start tomorrow?"

"You *are* serious."

"Peter's good with the plants. But he treats people like they're just another root vegetable. With the falloff in business, I need someone who's good with the customers, especially to push our living Christmas trees. We've been setting them up for seniors—bringing them in, taking them out after the holidays. Now, I'm thinking we ought to make the same offer to any customers. It's not just for business. You know how I feel about living Christmas trees."

Herb grinned. "One less tree needlessly chopped down."

"I'll meet you there at eight." Bret thought about the breakfast he needed to bring over to Sam. "Make that eight-thirty. Peter should have the nursery open by then, but I'm not counting on it."

"Aren't you staying for dinner?"

Bret grinned. "The way Janie was waving that spatula at the kids, I'm sure it'll be a gourmet feast, but I'll pass."

"Coward."

"You betcha."

"Hey, Bret." Herb's gaze turned soberly sincere. "Thanks."

"Sure."

The next morning Bret took a critical look at the crude porch ramp at Sam's house. It wasn't very attractive, but it was sturdy. The temporary threshold adapter he'd fashioned out of a few pieces of wood worked. And it would do until the one he'd ordered from the hardware store arrived.

He rang the bell, then tried the door. Since it was unlocked, he walked in. "Sam? I've got your breakfast."

Dropping the breakfast on the dining room table, he headed into the kitchen. Wasn't any easier to look at.

Charred black, the remains of the cabinets no longer resembled their original design. He could replace them with something easy that wasn't nearly as beautiful, but he was fond of Sam's parents. When he and Sam had dated, they'd treated him like a son. And they were always kind when he saw them at church, or anywhere in town. He sensed they felt guilty about the way Sam had ended the engagement.

Rolling toward the table, she looked at him tentatively when he walked back into the dining room.

"Do you know if your parents have any pictures taken in the kitchen?"

"Good morning to you, too." Sam glanced at the ignored food. "I imagine there are some pictures. We always had lots of suppers at the kitchen table."

"Where do you think the pictures are?"

"Um. Good question." She turned toward the built-in bookcases flanking the tall, wide fireplace, craning her head to see. "Mom has some albums there."

Knowing she couldn't reach that high, Bret searched the shelves.

"The leather-bound album to your right," Sam directed. "That one should be full of pictures."

He pulled the volume down, then carried it to the dining room table. "Let's take a look."

Although Sam wasn't accustomed to navigating her

wheelchair, after a few tries she got in place at the table. Bret picked up one of the dining room chairs and placed it next to her. "Okay, let's see what we've got."

As the pages of the book turned, the years fell away. Shots of Sam's family were bittersweet memories. Many of the photos captured the closeness of brother and sister.

Sam gently touched a picture of Andy standing alone, proudly showing off his Eagle Scout award.

Bret swallowed. Andy had been an example to him as well. Three years older than he and Sam, Andy had been the golden boy, destined to do good. From early on, Andy knew he wanted to be a teacher so that he could improve the fates of underprivileged kids. While in high school, he'd volunteered for a summer in Africa. He fell in love with the land and its people. He decided to return, to build a school and make sure "his" kids had better lives. But five years earlier, a doomed flight during a monsoon had ended his life and his dreams. Until his parents stepped in to make them happen.

Glancing surreptitiously at Sam, he swallowed.

Head down, hands covering her cheeks, she was trying to hide her tears.

Remnants of feelings he'd long put aside stirred. Despite them, he couldn't abandon her. Not until she recovered her once unstoppable tenacity. Then he could walk away, forget she'd returned.

Bret turned a page—to a photo of himself and Sam at college graduation with grins as wide as the state of

Texas. The picture hit him like a fist to the gut. Back then, full of youthful optimism, he'd been sure she would reconsider leaving Rosewood. He'd believed it until she boarded the bus out of town.

"Were we ever that young?" she asked in a quiet voice.

Bret knew he couldn't give in to his own emotions. "We're not exactly approaching Methuselah time."

Sam laughed, a humorless, brittle sound.

Silence blared between them. Feeling the tension in every muscle, Bret flipped another page in the album. The lone sound of it turning echoed. Unwilling to look at Sam, he studied the photos, then turned another page. And saw a picture taken in the kitchen. "Here's one." He tapped the photo. "We can get this enlarged for detail. It's a good angle on the cabinets."

She looked down. "I've been thinking about what you said. And you're right. I can't expect people I haven't seen in years to help me. It's a massive project and—"

"Did your parents have any renovations done since this picture?"

"I don't think so." Distracted, she shook her head. "Mom was always talking about upgrading, but she didn't want to lose her cabinets."

Sitting close to Sam, he felt the brush of her arm, the accidental graze of her hands as she reached for the album. Not moving, his gaze slid sideways. Her creamy ivory skin was just as he remembered. And the way her dark hair fell forward, just brushing her cheek. Wanting to sweep it back, to feel the softness of her cheek, he stood up abruptly.

As soon as possible, he'd hand over the responsibility for the kitchen to someone in her family. They could find the volunteers, get the renovations going. Without worrying what Sam's presence would do to them.

Startled by his sudden movement, Sam looked up at him.

Bret paced the floor, deliberately not looking at her. "I've talked to Matt Whitaker. He's agreed to work on the cabinets." Matt was a local artisan who designed furniture and other works of wood so remarkable he had a national following.

"His work is beautiful," she agreed. "But since he's become famous—"

"Nobody in Rosewood gets so famous they can't help a neighbor."

She swallowed.

Making himself study the photo and not Sam, Bret held it up to the light. "So, what did your mother *not* want that's in the kitchen now?"

"A fire."

Her wit had always captivated him. Nearly as much as the way her blue eyes could deepen, then capture him and not let go.

"Bret?"

He brought himself back to the planet with a jerk. "Yeah. Um, she still want a table in there or something more modern like an island?"

Samantha pushed the midnight-colored hair from her forehead. "She said something about updating, modernizing the kitchen, but not losing the integrity

of the house's time period. I know she wants a refrigerator that doesn't stick out any farther than the
counters and a bigger stove in an alcove sort of thing."

Bret glanced at the destroyed appliances. "I think
we can work new ones into the plan."

"Seems like she had some magazines set aside with
pictures of what she likes…"

Resisting an urge to look through the entire photo
album and find more pictures of himself and Sam
together, he dropped the photo on the table. "I've got
to get over to the nursery."

She looked confused. "But your breakfast…"

He grabbed the container. "I've got a new employee
starting today—my brother-in-law, Herb. Can't keep
him waiting."

"Well—"

"I'll try to get by this evening to wreck out some of
the kitchen."

"Okay, I'll—"

Fleeing, Bret didn't wait to hear her reply. From the
disquieting trickle of sweat traveling down his back,
he knew he didn't dare.

Chapter Four

Bret parked in the nursery lot, immediately seeing Herb's small truck, but not Peter's car. Fuming under his breath, he met his brother-in-law at the front. "See what I mean about Peter?" He unlocked the door. "I have a key for you in the office. Looks like you'll use one more than Peter does."

Herb tried to keep his expression neutral.

"It's okay." Bret flipped on the lights. "You can say what you think."

"Nope. Too soon for me to have an opinion."

"Won't take long," Bret muttered.

And it didn't take long, either, for a tour of all the nooks and crannies of the old main building.

"I'll show you the outbuildings later."

"Funny how you don't notice everything when you're just browsing." Herb studied the rows and rows of herbs that stretched out in one screened area. "Looks like I've got a lot to learn."

"After I show you the cash register, we'd better do your paperwork—W-4 and the lot the government requires."

The bell jangled on the front door and Peter strolled inside.

Glancing at his watch, Bret noted the time. He intended to keep track of it so he didn't have any issues about Peter's probation and its likely outcome.

Giving Herb time to finish the forms, Bret made a pot of coffee. By the time it brewed, Peter emerged from the back.

"Peter, you've probably seen Herb here before."

His assistant manager shrugged. "Lot of people come in here."

"Herb's starting today."

That got Peter's attention.

Herb extended his hand. Peter ignored him.

Bret counted silently to ten. "Herb will be working more on the inside. But he needs to learn everything."

Sullenly, Peter stared at Herb without replying.

Pulling the spare key from his pocket, Bret handed it to Herb.

"Hey." Peter's face mottled into an ugly shade of red. "You didn't give me a key until everybody else left."

"I can trust Herb," Bret replied briefly, not feeling any need for explanations.

"You friends?" Peter questioned.

"Not that it's your concern, but Herb's my brother-in-law."

A sarcastically knowing expression flooded Peter's harsh features. "Oh. Great. I'm on probation and all of a sudden, your *brother-in-law*'s working here?" He snorted. "And you making out like it was 'cause I was late yesterday when all the time you were planning on hiring him."

"Your work record speaks for itself. And for what it's worth, you pushed me over the edge yesterday. I was more inclined to fire you than give you a warning."

"You taking back the probation?"

Bret frowned. "No. You either shape up or you're out."

"Like it's going to be a fair test. Keep me on or your relative!" Slinking away, Peter muttered something unintelligible.

"That went well," Herb commented. "I'd forgotten how fun orientation day is."

"He'd have found out soon enough you're family."

Herb clapped one hand on Bret's shoulder. "Well, brother, any more benefits like that and I'll be spoiled for any other job."

Despite himself, Bret grinned. "It's going to be good having you around."

"Remember that when I mix up the petunias and the pansies."

If that was the worst he had to worry about, Bret would consider himself a lucky man.

It was late by the time Bret managed to get back to Sam's. Herb was intelligent, filled with initiative, but still, a full day of training was tiring. Not to mention all the hostility from Peter.

So he wasn't in a very talkative mood. "Let's split the work. You look for the magazines with the stuff your mother likes. I'll wreck out the old kitchen."

"Oh, that sounds fair." Before starting the search, Sam trailed him down the hall toward the kitchen, flinching when she looked at the scorched remains. "The counter was so beautiful."

"Old as the house is, the limestone was probably quarried close by. And the counters might have been redone when they modernized the kitchen. Means we can try and get a close match. I can borrow a tile saw and we'll cut off a piece for comparison."

She blinked. "You can do that?"

"Most of us can do a lot more than we think we can."

Her eyes, still wounded, met his. "I used to believe that."

Wishing she didn't have the ability to pull him in with a single look, he pushed aside old feelings. "It's time you started believing again."

"Easy for you to say," Sam muttered, pivoting back toward the living room.

She'd barely started down the hall when the door-bell rang.

Bret listened. When Sam didn't open the door, he laid down his tools and went to the entry hall.

Rachel stood on the porch, peering into the living room. "I was beginning to think Sam wasn't home."

"Which is impossible since she won't leave the house," Bret replied wryly.

Rachel rolled her eyes. "I've been trying to drag her to see the doctor and she won't budge."

"You have something set up?"

"Not much point until she agrees to go."

Bret pursed his lips. "Maybe we need to do it the other way around."

"You willing to help me on this?" Rachel asked hopefully.

He was going to find some duct tape and seal his mouth closed. "I could talk to J.C." J. C. Mueller was Rosewood's only neurologist and a friend of Bret's.

Impulsively Rachel hugged him. "That would be perfect!"

Yep, just perfect.

Samantha finished brushing her hair, then looked in the mirror. She'd never put much value on looks, but it was startling to see her near-skeletal reflection. Bret had always claimed she was beautiful. Sam peered closer. If that *had* been true, it certainly wasn't anymore. The unflattering clothes didn't help. Her wardrobe these days was sweats, the only thing she could struggle into on her own.

Bret would probably be by soon. She hadn't wanted to accept his help these last few weeks, but the truth was she couldn't have gotten by on her own much longer. Without asking, he'd installed grab bars in the bathroom and bought a shower chair so she could bathe. Rachel had taken over, adding vanilla shampoo and green-tea-scented bath gel, along with loads of thick, soft towels. Her cousin had also taken care of the laundry.

Between goodies from Ethel Carruthers and child-hood favorites Rachel brought over, Samantha had more than enough food. But she still shared breakfast from the café with Bret. He told her it was the only way he could be sure she really ate at least one meal a day. She heard him knock on the front door that she'd left unlocked for him. As had become his habit, he walked directly to the dining room table. "Change of pace today. Breakfast sandwiches."

She joined him.

He unfolded the paper from his own. "Less mess."

"Good idea." Her appetite was still nonexistent and she ate only a few bites. Bret finished his sandwich almost as quickly, surprising her. She glanced up. "You must be in a hurry."

"You could say that." He wiped his mouth with a paper napkin.

She noticed that he hadn't brought any coffee. He rarely went anywhere without a cup. He liked the brew so strong it was almost espresso. "I can't believe you forgot your coffee."

"Have my thermos in the Blazer, along with some cups." His chair scraped over the wooden floor as he pushed it back. "We have to get on the road."

Her face fell. "What?"

"You haven't been out of the house enough. You need fresh air."

Feeling panicked, Samantha shook her head. "I get plenty of air through the windows."

Bret grasped the handles of her chair. "Nope."

Before she could protest more, he pushed her out the door over the newly installed threshold adapter that had arrived the previous day. "Bret, wait! I don't want to go around the neighborhood."

"Good. We're taking a drive."

"A *drive*?"

"You know." He opened the passenger door of his SUV. "That thing when you get in the car and go somewhere."

Shaking her head, she reached for the wheels to reverse. But he was faster, lifting her up and into the vehicle. "Bret!"

Closing her door, he stowed her wheelchair in the back, then got inside.

"Where are we going?"

"Breathe, Sam."

She hadn't realized she was holding her breath in a death grip that nearly matched the one she had on the door handle.

"Have I ever done anything to hurt you?"

Never. "You used to be the master of practical jokes."

He turned the key, starting the car. "And you weren't?"

Sam felt like a bat pulled out of its cave, blinking in the sunlight, wanting desperately to be back in the safety of her parents' home.

"It's not far," he continued.

Nothing was very far in the small Hill Country town. Established in the mid-eighteen-hundreds, Rosewood had never outgrown its practical roots. Resisting the urge to become a tourist destination, instead it was a community that thrived on small businesses and individuality.

When Samantha had arrived, she hadn't paid attention to the cozy warmth of Main Street with its Victorian buildings and shops. Nor had she noticed the signs of summer in the large elm trees that lined the sidewalks. When she was a kid, superstores had tried to establish a foothold, but the town hadn't wanted to give up its rural lifestyle or run entrepreneurs out of business. Since the land outside town was owned by ranchers whose places had been in their families for generations, developers got nowhere with them either.

The town had invested in state-of-the-art hospital facilities, though. One that Bret was turning into. Dread assailed her. "What are you doing?"

Bret didn't reply until he found a parking spot near the physicians' building. "This is Rosewood, not Deadwood. We have doctors, indoor bathrooms, most everything."

Samantha bristled at his tone. She might have left eight years ago, but she didn't dislike her hometown. *"Really?"*

"And you have to keep up your medical care."

Sam hated that her emotions were now so close to

the surface that she felt like crying nearly all the time. "I told you I can't afford it."

Bret turned off the car, then faced her. "Sam, do you remember anybody in Rosewood going without care?"

It was the way they did things. When someone didn't have enough money, people donated services and whatever else they could to make certain no one was denied help. But she'd been away from that kind of thinking for a lot of years. Straining desperately not to cry, she leaned back, scrunching into her door. "I'm not going to be a charity case."

"That's okay by me." He retrieved the wheelchair, and rolled it to the passenger side. "You'd better lean in if you don't want to land on the ground."

Only the possibility of further humiliation made her move.

His hands were strong as he again lifted her. For a moment she wanted to wrap her arms around his neck and hang on. But she knew he wouldn't want her to. He hadn't wanted anything to do with her since their last and ultimate fight over the future.

Bret eased her into the chair, then took control of the handles. "The good part about going to therapy is once you get out of this chair, no one can push you around."

Yeah. That was going to happen. She was silent as they entered the building, then traveled through the corridors.

"You remember J. C. Mueller?" Bret asked. "Three years ahead of us in school?"

J.C. had been in Andy's class. "So he made it to medical school?"

"He's a neurologist. Gave up several offers to practice in New York, Chicago, Dallas." Bret slowed down at the elevators, backing her into an open one.

Samantha remained quiet as they reached the doctor's office and Bret signed her in. The consultation was pointless since she couldn't afford to follow through on anything J.C. suggested. But Bret wasn't listening.

It wasn't long before the nurse ushered them into an examination room. Before Sam could think of a way to escape, J.C. entered. His grin was as friendly as she remembered. "Samantha!"

She also remembered her manners. "J.C."

Instead of reaching for the chart hanging on the back of the door, he eased into the chair next to her, meeting Samantha at eye level. "So. Bret's dragged you here and you're wishing he hadn't."

Briefly glancing up at Bret, she swallowed. "Looks like you have the picture."

"I'd know more about the picture if you'll agree to let me send for your records."

Twisting her hands together, she looked down, uncomfortable beneath the two masculine gazes.

"Sam, if I'd gone into medicine to make money, I wouldn't have come back to Rosewood."

Embarrassment colored her pale cheeks. "So Bret told you."

"Glad he did. I never have understood why people will accept friendship, gifts, help with things out of their scope of experience, but they balk when it comes to money. I don't have a lot of money to give, but I can offer my expertise."

Overwhelmed, she covered her eyes with one hand.

"So, what do you say?"

Reluctantly, she uncovered her eyes. "It won't do any good, J.C. I tried to tell Bret. There's not any hope."

"Hope's a funny thing. The Lord surprises us when we least expect it." He reached for the chart. "One thing is certain—we can't know until we explore all the options." He extended a clipboard that held a request for transfer of medical records.

Bret leaned down, his mouth close to her ear. "You don't have to do this alone. Your family knows."

Shakily, she accepted the clipboard and pen, scribbling her name on the bottom of the paper. Drained, she slumped back.

"This is a good start," J.C. assured her.

Samantha didn't believe him. Maybe he'd had offers from New York, but she'd seen city doctors. She'd *heard* their opinions.

"My nurse will call in the request today. Shouldn't be long until we get the records. In the meantime, I'm recommending both aqua and physical therapy."

"It won't do any good." What physical therapy she'd tried in New York had failed.

"It won't hurt. In cases like yours, muscles atrophy. Even if the spine heals, the muscles can't respond after months of disuse. That's where therapy comes in." He patted her shoulder reassuringly. "Bret knows where the pool is, so you can get started."

She whipped her head up. *"Now?"*

"Can't think of a better time."

Bret held out his hand. "Thanks, J.C."

The doctor stood, accepting Bret's handshake. "Don't let her buffalo you into leaving."

Samantha stared. *"What?"*

"I know how intimidating you can be. I ran against you for student council, remember?"

She'd won. Back when everything was easy.

Bret wheeled Samantha to the physical therapy area despite her nonstop protests.

"This is ridiculous. I can't do any kind of water therapy wearing sweats."

He drew his eyebrows together in a frown. "Excellent point. Good thing Rachel's here with your stuff to change into."

Samantha twisted her head and Rachel rushed over with a tremulous smile. "Hey."

"Et tu?" Sam rubbed her forehead. "Plotting with Bret?"

"And J.C.," Rachel admitted. "You know we can't stand by and do nothing."

Hands folded in her lap, Samantha lifted her face. "I appreciate all the concern…I know it's because you care. But it really, *really* is a waste of time to try and make this work."

"It's our time," Rachel rebuked gently.

Outnumbered and weary, Sam gave in. "I didn't pack a swimsuit."

Rachel took Bret's place behind the chair. "We do have stores in Rosewood."

As they headed to the women's dressing room, Bret retrieved his gym bag from the men's lockers. He'd left it there after he and J.C. had come up with a plan. Rachel had figured out all the details for clothes, along with a time that worked for both of them.

Changing into his own knee-length swim shorts, he glanced at his watch. He should be at the nursery, but Herb would do his best.

With J.C.'s blessing, Bret and Rachel intended to learn how to do the water exercises. The aqua therapy teacher, Wanda, was willing to teach them so Sam could have daily sessions. And there wasn't any charge to use the facilities. Once Rachel was comfortable with the exercises, he could turn the entire task over to her. It wasn't just the fact that he needed to be both at work and checking on his dad—this much proximity to Sam was a bad plan.

Guessing it would take the women longer to change, he stowed his clothes in the locker, then looped a towel around his neck. In time, they emerged, wearing matching T-shirts and shorts to cover their swimsuits, like many of the other patients. Sam looked like a well-covered but trapped animal.

He took the towel from his neck and tossed it on a bench. "Reminds me of the time you tried to push me in the pool, missed and fell in yourself."

Startled, Sam stopped fussing with her exposed calves. She was thin, but her legs were still knockouts. "I'm not even wet yet."

"Only a matter of minutes. There's a special PVC wheelchair and ramp to get you in."

Mortification filled her features.

He stepped closer. "Or we could just hop in ourselves." Not giving her time to process his words, he scooped her up, cradling her in his arms.

"What do—"

"We don't really need the special chair." She was so slight now, it was like carrying feathers. Feathers covered in silky skin. Skin that grazed his arms, teased his senses.

Instinctively she wrapped her arms around his neck to hold on. And he remembered how they'd felt in that same position years ago when they dated in college. He'd never expected to feel them there again. Nor to experience a rush of awareness now that they were.

Warm water enveloped them both as he walked deeper, stopping at one of the built-in ledges that Sam could sit on. Rachel followed, taking a spot directly across the pool.

The teacher wasn't far behind. "Hi. Samantha? I'm Wanda, the aqua therapy teacher. I hope you'll relax, let the water soothe you. We'll learn some exercises to rebuild your strength, but part of the therapy is to ease muscle tension."

Samantha averted her face. "That's not really a problem with my muscles."

"Dr. Mueller briefed me. You have a spinal injury and your legs aren't responding. Those muscles may be in a state of atrophy—I understand we'll know more after the doctor runs some tests. Naturally, the shock of injury causes tension in the rest of your body. Your neck, shoulders—the usual suspects."

Reluctantly, Samantha nodded. "I suppose so."

"Without an injury, I get stressed." Good at her job, Wanda had understanding in her voice without resorting to pity. "The warm water helps. Try to think of it as an oversize tub."

In just over waist-deep, Sam tentatively touched the surface of the water. It was a tiny step, but Bret expected most of them would be. J.C. had been candid when Bret had talked with him alone. It was possible Sam might never regain the use of her legs. Then again, she hadn't had the intensive program he thought she needed. After a long coma, her muscles hadn't worked properly. Not having a positive attitude about the therapy could have made a huge difference as well. And she hadn't been surrounded by friends, or the power of prayer.

Not letting the past intrude, Bret had placed Sam's name in the prayer circle a day after the fire. Now the entire church was praying for her. Sam didn't know it, but she was being circled herself—neighbors and friends wanting to shore her up, to help in any way they could. Despite the untenable break in their relationship, Bret hated that Sam had been injured, that she'd lost hope.

Listening closely, he followed as Wanda took them through some relaxation motions. Warm water slipped between them, pushing them apart, pulling them back together. The entire time his hand remained at Sam's waist, to support her, he told himself. Even though his heart echoed a time he believed they'd never be separated.

Chapter Five

"You've got to tell your parents." Rachel ladled out more of the homemade soup she'd brought over.

Samantha shook her head. "Your mother's already making chicken soup for me. Imagine what my mom would do."

Rachel sniffed the broth. "My mother does make good soup."

"Which you prefer to a hamburger? Right." Samantha accepted the mug and took a small sip.

"I'd hate to be you when they find out."

Sam put the mug on the tabletop. "Too many people are already in on my secret. Someone's bound to talk. And then they'll be back here." In Rosewood, where she couldn't put them off or hide away in an apartment. She loved them more than she could say, but she couldn't bear the pain in their eyes. More pain than one set of parents should have to endure. "I'm just not ready."

Rachel's expression softened. "Sam, I don't know

how you feel…how I'd feel in your place. But I'm sure you can conquer this." She leaned forward. "You're the most determined person I've ever known. You've always run the fastest, the farthest."

Sam couldn't contain a brittle laugh.

"Running isn't just physical," Rachel insisted. "Your mind has to be in sync…you have to believe."

"Belief isn't on the agenda anymore."

"Do you remember when we were eight? You wanted to climb the Hyde Plateau?" She laughed at the memory. "Andy was older, stronger and you still talked him into racing to the top. None of us could believe you won, but you acted like there couldn't have been any other outcome."

"I'm not eight anymore." Determined not to become a pity case, Sam left the rest of the difference unsaid.

"How many people insisted you'd never discover a new species? That everything had already been cataloged?"

"I…" Stumbling for a reply, her protest died away.

"Yes? This is different?" Rachel stood, pacing across the wooden floor. "Sure it is. And how much more is at stake?"

Sam found her voice. "Splashing around in aqua therapy's going to change things?"

"Sitting in your chair will?" Rachel knelt next to the wheelchair, then squeezed Sam's hand, her expression encouraging. "You know I'm not going to give up on this. Bret won't either."

Startled, Sam drew back. "Bret?"

"Don't let the past get in the way. He isn't."

"No." Samantha hadn't seen a glimpse of the feelings she'd once shared with him. He acted as though they'd just been casual acquaintances. "He's not."

Rachel checked the contents of her gym bag, making sure she had everything they needed. "Have you made any progress with that broth?"

Samantha ignored the still full mug, looking for another way to distract her cousin. "You can't keep taking off this much time from your job."

"Bret and I have it worked out. For now, we'll alternate taking you to the pool. After I've learned the aqua stuff well enough, I'll get someone else to help us. Until we get reinforcements, we'll split the regular therapy sessions, too. Mom wants to help, but I'm worried about her rheumatoid arthritis. The latest treatment hasn't been all that successful—and she hates taking the shots. She could go with you to the water therapy class, but I'm not sure she'd be much help. At home, Dad helps *her* in and out of the hot tub."

"But—"

"If you don't cooperate, I have Bret standing by."

He was outside, waiting to talk with Matt about the kitchen cabinets. Samantha didn't want to go to therapy, but she wanted a confrontation with Bret less.

It was the futility of the therapy that disturbed her. Sure, she'd heard of people who overcame the odds—walking despite doctors' predictions. But she hadn't made an iota of progress. Something she couldn't get across to anyone. And she hated being mollycoddled as though she were mentally incapacitated as well.

"Sam?"

Her energy faded, and along with it, her defiance. "Whatever."

"That's the spirit," Rachel teased.

Between them, Sam may have been the tenacious one, but Rachel had always been the cheeriest. There were more giggles than grinches in her world. Maybe that's why they'd always gotten on so well. No matter what Sam thought up, Rachel figured out a way to make it fun. But Samantha was convinced this stupid therapy was going to blotch her cousin's pristine record.

Once Sam was outside, Bret lifted her into the car, noting the mutiny on her face, trying to ignore the effect of her soft limbs in his arms. "No apple for the teacher?"

She thinned her lips even more. "Isn't it enough that I'm going?"

Seeing she was safely inside, he closed the door, then packed her chair in the back. One of the aides at the hospital would help Rachel with Sam, getting her in and out of the car.

It was an important day. J.C. had received many of Sam's records from New York, and he also had results from the tests done locally. Based on the combination, he had assigned a physical therapist, Harold, to her case.

J.C. and Harold put together a comprehensive program of treatments and exercises meant to rebuild her body, concentrating on the atrophied leg muscles.

Bret guessed Sam's stubbornness was because she didn't dare believe the program could work. If she didn't believe, didn't hope, she wouldn't be devastated if the therapy failed.

As they drove off, he spotted his friend Matt Whitaker approaching in a Dodge Ram pickup. Matt designed all things wooden, including furniture—pieces so unique collectors around the country waited in line for his work. But true to his hometown roots, he donated both his time and some of his creations to Rosewood fundraisers. And he hadn't hesitated when Bret had asked for help with the kitchen.

"That Samantha with Rachel?" Matt asked, stepping down from the tall truck. "Looks different."

"She's thin." *Skinny as a stick, actually.* A concern he'd tried to push to the back of his mind.

"Leah makes a killer homemade pizza—West coast style," Matt offered, referring to his wife, who was from California. "I know she'd be glad to bring one over."

"Sam just won't eat much." Bret shrugged. "J.C. thinks it's depression. By the time she woke up from the coma, her appetite had disappeared."

Matt's gaze skipped to the front of the house. "I must have spent half my childhood here."

Bret saw the knot in Matt's throat. Must be thinking about Andy.

"I thought Andy was invincible. Stupid."

"Normal," Bret disputed. "Friends aren't supposed to die when they're young."

Matt swallowed again.

And Bret thought of Matt's younger brother, John, who had also died at a young age. It was a lot of hurt. "We found some old pictures of the kitchen. Scanned, then enlarged them for detail."

Nodding, Matt walked with him toward the front door. "I remember the woodwork pretty well. Saw the Shaws..." He paused. "Would have been right before they left for Africa. We had pie in the kitchen, like we'd done a million times before. Don't forget cabinets like those. Made of native pine. Not easy to find, but I can get hold of some."

"Lot of carving on the old ones."

"Yep. Mrs. Shaw said her grandfather designed them."

Bret knew his friend was purposely concentrating on the specifics of the job rather than the feelings he must be experiencing. When Matt's brother, John, had been killed in a car accident, he had left his baby son, Danny, with Matt. But Matt hadn't known that John had run off with the child. It had taken eight years for Leah, Danny's mother, to find him. Now they were a happy family, but it had taken plenty of heartache to get to a good place.

Maybe he shouldn't have pulled him in on this project. "Matt...I don't want this to stir up bad memories. I can get a carpenter to help."

Matt shook his head. "It was bad when Andy died—made me think about old...stuff. But the Shaws mean a lot to me. I want to do this."

Bret nodded in understanding.

"How 'bout you? Being around Sam this much?"

Bret didn't want to go there. "She's an old friend."

"Uh-huh."

Ignoring the disbelief in Matt's voice, Bret led the way down the hall. Even though he'd wrecked out a lot of the damaged materials, he knew it was a shock seeing the destruction for the first time.

Matt stopped short, staring through the tall, arched doorway to the kitchen. Slowly he shook his head. "If this thing had spread…Sam might not have made it."

The unexpected blow to his gut silenced Bret. Trailing his friend, he watched as Matt took in the scene, ran his hands over the small bit of wood left on one wall. And the whole time he mentally echoed Matt's sentiment. Sure, he had known the fire was dangerous. Stupid, he'd thought at the time. Careless. But he hadn't let himself wander to Matt's conclusion.

Matt crouched down, examining the floor. "Even this is scorched."

Bret gestured to a gaping hole covered by thick-gauge plastic. "The window blew out, so there was plenty of air to feed the fire."

Standing back up, Matt nodded in understanding. "And by the time Sam could get to her phone…"

"Good thing you got here so fast." Matt inclined his head toward the front. "Saw the ramp you built."

"Not pretty, but it works."

"You want to tell me why the Shaws can't know Sam's back?"

Bret explained her reasoning. "It won't last. The

whole town can't keep that kind of secret. And it's already getting out."

"Wouldn't be such a bad thing if her folks came home."

"Sam thinks it's selfish—her taking them away from the school." Bret shook his head. "But she's smart enough to realize they'll find out, then come home at some point."

"Yeah." Matt stared around the destroyed room. "Lot of good times in here. You, too."

Bret swallowed.

"Lots of good times," Matt repeated slowly. He exhaled, then met Bret's eyes squarely. "If this is hard for me, it must be killing you."

Samantha loved early mornings. From her eight weeks of therapy, she was strong enough to wheel herself over the threshold adapter, then onto the wrap-around porch that ran the length of house. The spindled banister was low enough that she could see over the carved railing.

Theirs was a Queen Anne–style Victorian, with towers, turrets, bay windows and fanciful detailing. Luckily, one of the first-floor rooms had been converted to a bedroom with an en suite bathroom for Samantha's grandmother.

She breathed in deeply. Scents from the last of the season's roses blended with the morning dew. She had missed this uniquely Hill Country smell. Not everyone associated particular odors of nature with locales. But since she had worked outdoors all over the world, she'd come to recognize how very different the aromas were. She relished the memories of childhood the familiar scent evoked. It had been a good one, she acknowledged. A childhood filled with laughter and love.

She glanced at the wide steps that led down to the sidewalk. Swallowing, Samantha remembered skipping up them without a care. Glancing off to the right, she studied the ramp Bret had built.

Of all the people in Rosewood, he was the last one Samantha would have expected to be helping her. He hadn't even attended Andy's funeral service. Her mother had said something about him being on a buying trip. But she'd taken it as a personal rebuff.

The day she had broken their engagement flickered in her mind. She'd honestly thought Bret would find a way to follow her. And she couldn't give up an opportunity to intern with one of the world's most accomplished plant pathologists. But Bret hadn't understood. Had never forgiven her.

Sam blinked at a sudden flash of light. Sunshine reflected off Bret's SUV as he turned into the driveway. Once they had been so in sync that she wouldn't have thought it odd to suddenly see Bret at the exact moment she was thinking about him.

He climbed out of the driver's side, retrieved their breakfast, then strolled lazily up the walk. "You're up and around early."

Sam shrugged, trying to shake off the memories.

"Thought maybe we could eat breakfast here on the porch." Rocking chairs flanked the large double door entry. Even though the veranda in back had a dining table, it wasn't easy to access since the fire.

"Good thing I got breakfast sandwiches." He pulled up one of the small ceramic-topped tables. They were used mostly in the summer, when the heat drew the Shaws outside to tall glasses of lemonade or iced tea.

Bret wiped off the table with a paper napkin, then used the bag as a makeshift cover to set the sandwiches and coffee thermos on.

"Coffee always smells best in the early morning," Samantha mused.

His dark-brown eyes flickered in surprise. But a moment later they were steady, guarded.

She picked up a packet of sugar and emptied it in the steaming brew. "I've been thinking about something."

He lifted his eyebrows.

"Am I taking too much of your work time…getting breakfast?"

He paused. "Trying to get rid of me?"

"Of course not." Now nervous, she stirred the sugar.

Bret stopped unwrapping his sandwich. "Speaking of work—you never have told me the details about your accident."

She stirred the sugar more vigorously, remembering the brief bit she'd told him the first day after the fire.

"Unless you're trying to melt the plastic stir stick, I think your coffee ought to be mixed by now."

"Oh!" Flustered, she retrieved the slender, straw-like stirrer. "Of course." But she didn't lift the cup.

"The accident," Bret prodded.

"I was restoring a Georgian garden in upstate New York. The house had been neglected for years and the garden was in even worse shape. New owners were renovating the entire estate. And they wanted the garden to shine like it had in the 1700s. The basic layout was still there. But it was completely over-grown. I located the original design, found that the old sundial was missing. I'd brought in extra labor—muscles to shift the heavy stuff and demolish a horrible building that had been added.

"I wanted to check the progress from an elevated perspective. So I climbed up to the top balcony of the old carriage house. Like I told you, there'd been a freak snowstorm the day before. I didn't think anything of it, but the snow had melted, then frozen in the night. Black ice, it's called. I stepped out on the balcony, slid like I was rocket-propelled. And I landed on the brick pavement more than a story below." She stopped abruptly.

"And then?"

"There wasn't any *then*. I was in a coma for months. Don't remember anything after I fell until I woke up."

He lifted his egg-and-bacon sandwich, took a bite, then chewed slowly.

Sam couldn't manage even a sip of coffee.

Bret swallowed, then reached for his cup, his face tightening.

"What?" She asked, unable to keep the words in. "I can tell you want to say something."

He put down the sandwich, wiped his hands together, then firmed his jaw. "When you left, you said it was so you could discover new species. What were you doing restoring a garden?"

Her mouth gaped open. "It happens to be a very important historical garden. And some of it was at risk. Takes a plant pathologist to diagnose, then treat the problem. Besides, I've done more than my share of exploring, discovering."

"I've seen your name in journals." His eyes turned accusing. "Didn't know it was about getting famous."

Some of her old spirit revived. "You know it wasn't ever about that. You were content here. I needed more."

He grabbed his sandwich, crumpled the uneaten portion up with the paper it had been wrapped in, then balled the mess into one fist. "If you want your kitchen fixed, don't go down this road."

"You brought it up!" she protested.

Standing, Bret strode across the porch, each booted footstep loud, defined.

"Where are you going?"

"Out back." His words were clipped as he stomped down the steps.

"But—"

"Drop it, Sam."

Swallowing, she stared after him. The smell of the cooling coffee mixed with the Hill Country scent. But her memories were no longer nostalgic. Instead, all she could absorb was the anger in Bret's eyes. And the sinking realization that the love he'd once felt for her was gone.

Chapter Six

Unable to cool off, Bret finished up at Sam's, then sped over to the nursery. When he arrived, Bret was surprised to see that Herb was stocking shelves, per Peter's instructions, mixing plant foods with the insecticides.

"I didn't think it made good sense," Herb explained. "But Peter knows a lot more about this stuff than I do."

"There's a diagram of the store layout on the computer. It's tied in with the ordering system. Have you gotten into that program yet?"

Herb shook his head.

"With your experience, you'll be able manage it blindfolded. It's fine by me if you take over responsibility for the computer. Just don't make it too hard for me to relearn." Bret gestured to a display near the rear of the store. "All the insecticides and weed killers are kept in the back. I encourage people to use natural alternatives, so I don't want them to grab a bag of chemicals when they first step in the store." Bret walked over to a stand of books and pulled one out. "This is a guide about natural methods. When it's slow, read up on the methods."

Herb lifted his eyebrows in mild reproof. "I can handle reading it at home. And you don't have to treat me with kid gloves."

"Don't want to take advantage of you, either."

Herb set the book on the counter. "Right now I've got some sacks to shift."

Pleasant change. Someone offering to work instead of sulking because he had to. On a personal level, Bret still missed the employees who had retired, having known them his entire life. But they'd also kept the mood light, not to mention that he'd never once had to check on their work.

Herb passed him with a flatbed dolly. "Looks like you sat in a bed of fire ants this morning. Something else wrong?"

Plenty. But his brother-in-law had enough problems of his own. "Got up on the wrong side of the bed. Think I'll go check on Dad now."

"Okay. Did you think about what I said? Changing the computer password?"

Bret pressed the palm of one hand against his forehead. "Completely forgot."

Herb frowned. "You want me to try and come up with something?"

"Sure." Bret's mind wasn't on the computer, or anything in the business for that matter. "I won't be long."

* * *

It was early for the daily visit to his parents' house, but Bret couldn't get Sam's words out of his head. He needed to talk to someone who understood, never revealed a confidence and had a level head.

It wasn't a stretch to find his father in the greenhouse out back. In the early morning light, it seemed that Robert's face was paler than usual.

"Morning."

His father turned from the workbench. "Hello, son. I was just thinking about you, wondering how Herb's working out."

"Great. Not only because he's smart, and learns—" Bret snapped his fingers "—just like that. But he doesn't bite my head off."

"Peter at you again this morning?"

"Nah." Bret straddled a stool.

Robert snipped carefully. "Sam liking therapy any better?"

"Still have to drag her there, says it won't do any good."

"You think it might."

"She's already stronger."

"But that's not what's on your mind."

Bret shouldn't have been surprised. His dad had always seen straight to the heart of things. "No." Unable to sit still, he stood, pacing the narrow aisle, careful not to brush against any of the delicate blooms. "Just found out she got hurt restoring some fancy garden."

"Ah." Robert knew the history between Bret and Samantha.

"So much for leaving to discover new species."

Robert frowned. "I thought she found one."

"Yeah."

"What kind of garden was she working on?"

Bret described what Sam had told him, finishing sarcastically. "Said it was 'historically important.'"

"Sounds like it is. You've told me often enough that we're not just growers, we're conservators. And gardens that old take a specialist. They're just as important as preserving a historic building. Especially ones that date back to the Revolutionary War."

Bret sighed. "I suppose."

"But it's not what you thought she'd be doing when she left. Son, she probably didn't either." Robert paused. "I've seen the journals, too. Sam did what she set out to do. It's almost unheard of these days to locate a new species. Yet she did." Robert shifted, turning on his stool. "Not too long ago, I read that a rare bald songbird species was just found in Asia— the first time in more than a hundred years. In the interview, the naturalist said he'd been determined and wouldn't give up until he learned all he could about the species." Robert chuckled. "Doesn't that sound like Samantha? Tenacious, unstoppable. But plans change, grow, sometimes detour. You didn't plan on propagating living Christmas trees."

"No." But he'd stayed with the rest of his original plan.

"Main reason the nursery's still in business is

your foresight. Maybe you need to use a little more of it with Sam."

Bret stared at his father in surprise.

"You're looking at the past, not the present."

Swallowing, Bret paused. "So is she. That's why she won't try to get better."

"Two blind bulls locking horns." Robert took a deep breath. "Foresight's your gift, son."

"And you think I should use it." Bret felt the pain of the past conflicting with the knowledge of what was right. What the Lord would want him to do.

"I trust you, son."

Maybe. But Bret didn't trust himself.

For several days, the atmosphere when Bret stopped by with breakfast was uneasy. He wasn't rude, just quiet, closed down. So Samantha was completely taken aback when he told her they were going somewhere.

"But it's not time for therapy and I don't have a test scheduled today." Besides, she wasn't dressed for the hospital. She hadn't been able to find her sweats, forcing her to struggle into jeans.

The rolling of Bret's eyes was slight; still, she caught it.

"Do you have to argue about everything?" he asked.

"Me?" Remembering their last real conversation, her lips snapped shut.

Bret waited to see if she had more to say.

Biting her tongue, she refused to provoke another argument.

Apparently satisfied, he propped open the front door and wheeled her outside, down the ramp and to his Blazer.

Although Sam had gone through town to get to the hospital, she hadn't been past Rosewood's borders since she'd returned. And on the bus drive, she hadn't paid attention to the countryside, concentrating instead on just getting home.

Now, though, determined not to say the wrong thing, she studied the hillsides as though she'd never seen them before. Early autumn's imprint was settling in the trees, whistling through the long, wild grass—yellowing strands blended in with the green.

"I love this time of year when summer's almost over and fall's starting," she mused.

"Autumn's almost as good as spring." They shared a rare grin.

"You'd think we're both horticulturists," Sam added, enjoying the light moment.

His grin disappeared. "Yeah."

A conversation with Bret was about as easy as navigating a field of densely packed cacti. Turning her gaze back toward the window, she saw a herd of cattle sprawled across the winding acreage. A tall derrick stood in the center of the herd. Oil pumped steadily, the wide metal arm thrusting methodically into the earth. Cattle and oil. Nothing said Texas like they did.

Waves of memories assaulted her. The years her entire family had been intact. When her brother and grandparents were all alive. Days that had seemed to glide by. Yet she'd been so impatient to get on with life, to explore outside her small town. Unconsciously, she sighed.

"What?"

"Oh." Embarrassed that she'd uttered the involuntary sound aloud, she shrugged. "Nothing."

"Big sigh for nothing."

"Just thinking back…about Andy, my family."

His expression loosened. "Yeah. He was a good guy."

Sam wanted to ask why he hadn't come to her brother's funeral. She didn't, feeling as always that it was because of her.

They continued down the road tucked between hills and pastures. Gradually, she relaxed, lured as always by the late blooming wildflowers.

Bret turned with the curve of the road and Sam leaned in as well. Her shoulder touched his. Bret's eyes darted from the road to rest on her face. Her breath short, Sam felt his nearness, the hard muscles of his arm as he gripped the steering wheel. Somewhere in her thoughts, it flickered that she should remind him about watching the road. Her lips opened, but she didn't speak, instead falling into the gold-flecked depths of his eyes. She warmed beneath his gaze as it left her eyes to study her lips.

She lifted her chin ever so slightly, remembering the kisses they'd shared, the warming of her heart.

Wondering if he would lean closer, she felt a sharp jab of disenchantment as he jerked his gaze away to concentrate on his driving.

It was sensible, the right thing to do. And so disappointing she wanted to pound her hand on the armrest. Instead, she tried to appear as unaffected as he seemed.

Deliberately, she stared out the window with forced enthusiasm. Uncertain just how far they had come, Sam was surprised when Bret turned in at the Markham Ranch, wondering what they'd come for.

He passed the main house, heading toward the barn, where a man stood in the bed of a truck, unloading freshly baled hay. Bret waved at the man, then continued toward the stables, where he parked.

Curiosity ran amok. Bret didn't offer an explanation, instead retrieving her wheelchair and settling her in it. She noticed he didn't linger this time when he held her, releasing her as if she was a hot iron.

Samantha could hear the quiet neighing and whinnying of the horses as she and Bret approached the wide, propped-open doors. The clean smell of more bales of fresh hay punctuated the air.

Horses lifted their heads at the unfamiliar scents of two new people. Unexpectedly, Sam smiled. She had always loved horses. As a kid, she'd ridden as often as she could.

A chestnut mare whinnied and Bret pushed the wheelchair in the horse's direction.

Sam drew in her breath. "She's a beauty."

"I think so." Bret stopped in front of the stall.

A white star on the mare's forehead broke up the honeyed perfection of her silky coat. Ears pricked up, the mare stared with interest at Sam.

Sam itched to touch the star, to rub the horse's mane, run her hands down its muzzle. Forgetting for an instant, she tried to rise. Hating that she couldn't, Sam slumped back.

"Sam, this is Sugar."

Pushing the thoughts aside, Samantha smiled tremulously at the animal.

Bret pulled Sam's chair back, then opened the stall door as Sugar pawed the ground, eager to get out.

"Bret?"

Not answering, he picked up a rope that hung from a nail next to the stall, then looped it over Sugar's neck. When the rope was secure, he pulled a carrot from his back pocket and gave it to Samantha.

Nearly as eager as the horse, Sam offered the treat to the mare. Sugar delicately accepted the carrot, her manners as gentle as her appearance.

"I figured you two would get on."

Sugar bent her head down and Sam stroked her muzzle. Memories of riding with Bret in the long summer days surfaced. It had seemed the carefree seasons would last forever. That she would have him in her life always.

Minutes passed as Sam continued stroking the calm horse. Sunbeams pierced through the tall, open doors and dust motes floated in the air. It was so familiar, so comforting.

Bret handed Sam the rope and she glanced up at him surprise.

"Be right back."

Sugar didn't seem inclined to go anywhere, so Samantha tamped down a brief flare of panic. Holding the rope, she felt a few gentle tugs as Sugar moved her head, but nothing she couldn't control. *Imagine. Being in control.*

She swallowed.

The sound of solid bootsteps rang through the stable. Collecting herself, she saw Bret returning, holding a bridle.

"Are you planning to ride?"

He reached for the rope and tied it to a post. "Think I should?"

Longing filled her, but she batted it away, forcing enthusiasm into her voice. "Of course."

While she watched, he slid the bit into Sugar's mouth, then pulled the crown of the bridle over first one ear, then the other. After fastening the buckles, he straightened up the mare's blond mane, then smoothed a blanket over her back. He lifted up the saddle as though it weighed nothing. Sam couldn't miss the play of muscles beneath his cotton shirt, the endless length of his jeans-clad legs. Somehow, Bret was even more attractive than he'd been in college. Certainly as appealing. Definitely as captivating.

All tacked up, Sugar was ready to ride. However, Bret tied the reins to a post. "Ready?"

"For what?"

"Your ride." His voice was preposterously mild in comparison to his words.

"Right. Is she a jumper? I'd really excel at that."

Before she could grab the handles to hang on to her chair, Bret lifted her out. Cradled in his arms, Samantha felt the strength she'd just glimpsed. He stepped up on a crate beside the stall, then set her on the saddle, lifting one leg over the horn so that she settled correctly.

"What on earth are you doing?" Sam clutched Sugar's mane, hanging on for dear life.

Bret handed her the reins, then grasped the halter, leading Sugar outside. A man stood, holding the reins of a pinto.

"I don't know what you're up to," Sam hissed in a quiet voice, humiliation sweeping over her.

"Butch, would you hold on to Sugar?"

The older man nodded and switched places with Bret, who mounted the pinto.

Sam waited until Butch strolled away. "If you wanted to kill me, you could have just left me in the fire."

He snorted. "You'd think you'd never been on a horse."

"Not without working legs!" she retorted.

"Since you've been going to therapy, you have some movement in your hips."

A tiny bit. After weeks and weeks of therapy. And ever since, Rachel had carried on as though she'd suddenly begun to walk. Sam wasn't nearly as impressed, since her legs were still lifeless. Her therapists, Wanda and Harold, had insisted that it was an improvement. They had also insisted on increasing the work on her atrophied leg muscles. She even had homework—exercises to do while lying in bed, even some from her wheelchair.

"And I'll be right here in case you fall off."

"Gee, that's encouraging."

He grinned. "Chicken?"

Her competitive nature spurted. "Of course not." Sugar pawed the ground, and Sam's courage disappeared. Feeling the blood leave her face, she wondered if she might faint. Which wouldn't be such a bad thing. It would get her out of this. But she didn't pass out. "I...I haven't ridden in years."

His brusque expression relented a fraction. "I'm not going to let you get hurt, Sam. We'll take it real easy. You have a good hold on the horn?"

She nodded, afraid to speak in case her voice wobbled.

Leaning over, he took hold of Sugar's reins, then nudged his own horse forward.

Unable to grip with her knees, Samantha couldn't get a good seat on the horse. But as he'd promised, Bret kept the pace to a very slow walk, allowing her to clutch the saddle horn and hang on.

After the first terrifying steps, the butterflies in her stomach settled. The fear fading, Sam felt something she'd lost since the accident. Freedom. Moving without someone pushing her, without struggling to turn the wheels of her chair...

Hesitant to look away from her grip on the saddle, Sam quickly glanced up at Bret. So gruff and casual... To goad her into agreeing. Knowing, somehow, the way being astride the horse would make her feel.

A light breeze ruffled her hair, tickled her neck. And though the muscles didn't respond, she automatically tried to grip the horse with her knees. Harold and Wanda would be pleased.

While the pace remained sedate, Sam glanced up again from her grip on the horn to see where they were going. Bret kept to the flat area, rather than heading up the hills, where gravity wouldn't be her friend.

She had missed being outside, among the trees and plants she loved. And it was a wonder to look down on her surroundings rather than constantly craning her neck up to see. Funny how the little things could be missed so much. She used to begin every day with a walk, not always long, but quiet, so she could arrange the day ahead in her mind. Since the accident, she hadn't arranged anything other than her escape back to Rosewood.

Bret slowed his horse so that they rode side by side rather than in a line. "So how's it feel?"

"Just like you thought it would." Words seemed insufficient to express her gratitude. "How'd you happen on Sugar?"

"Markham's a friend. Haven't kept my own horse for a while now."

Samantha's own horse had always been kept at her grandparents' farm. After they had both passed away, she'd boarded Princess at a stable close to town until the mare died at a peaceful old age. "This is…really thoughtful."

Bret shrugged. "You need to remember how it

feels to be in control again, so you won't accept anything less."

She looked at the reins in his hands. Still, she had some control. And certainly freedom. "Bret...we haven't talked about it...but is there someone who might resent the amount of time you're spending with me?"

"Asking about my love life?"

Samantha blushed so deeply she could feel the warmth flooding her face. "I just don't want to be the cause of...well, any trouble."

"You're not."

He hadn't exactly clarified the situation. Was there a woman in his life? She itched to ask, but knew it wasn't a safe subject. Besides, there had to be. The women in Rosewood couldn't be that blind. "That's good. I'm glad you have someone so understanding."

He grunted.

She darted a glance at his face. Still not revealing anything. She used to be able to read his every expression, from the cleft in his chin to the smallest movement of his dark eyebrows. As for those mesmerizing eyes....

"What about you?"

Startled, she jerked, straightening her back and nearly losing her grip. "What about me?"

"If we're exchanging confidences..."

Unfortunately, she knew what he was asking. "I was always too busy to meet anyone." Sounded absurd in hindsight, Sam realized. "I dated, of course, but nothing serious." No one had ever lived up to Bret, she suddenly realized.

When she had first left Rosewood, her days were full, chasing her career. But even when she had free time, Samantha never found anyone she really cared for. How had she not seen that she was comparing each one to Bret?

He didn't comment, instead guiding the horses, watching the path. But Sam caught the tightening of his jaw.

It was too much to expect his reaction had anything to do with her. She'd thrown that expectation away when she left.

Chapter Seven

"Wow!" Rachel gazed at Sam in wonder. "You rode a *horse*?" She shook her head. "And all this time you've been telling me therapy's hardly done any good."

"*Rode* is an exaggeration. I told you. Bret led the horse and I just hung onto the saddle horn."

Rachel folded another towel, adding it to a stack of freshly washed laundry. "What a great idea. That Bret's a wonder."

Sam looked down at the floor. He was more than a wonder.

"But then you already know that." Rachel kept her gaze on the towels.

"Don't try to stir dead embers."

"I'm not the one who set the house on fire," Rachel retorted.

Samantha rolled her eyes. "It was an ingenious plan. Especially since I knew exactly who'd be volunteering that night."

Laughing, Rachel plumped another towel into a neat rectangle. "He's worth it."

They sat in comfortable silence as Rachel filled the basket with clean clothes. Friends forever, they didn't have to fill every moment with conversation. But Sam was surprised when her cousin sighed deeply.

"What's wrong?"

"Dad's been worried about keeping your secret." Rachel folded a sweatshirt. "Every time he talks to Uncle Ed and Aunt Joyce, they tell him that they only get letters from you now. And they're really concerned. He thinks your parents deserve to know you're home."

The weight of her secret had settled on too many people, Samantha realized. "I keep thinking they're going to find out any day now."

"They'd worry less if the news came from you." Rachel's large blue eyes were round with concern.

"You're probably right." She paused, staring out the living room window to the quiet street. "But I dread it."

Rachel clasped Sam's shoulder. "Your parents love you to pieces. It was hard for them when you left after college, but they got through it. They'll understand this, too."

Startled, Sam jerked her head up to search her cousin's gaze. She hadn't ever considered how much her leaving would bother them. They'd sent her off with good wishes and love. And, apparently, pain.

"You talked them into going back to Africa once you were in rehab," Rachel continued. "Do you honestly believe your parents will think it's worse for you to be here, surrounded by family and friends?"

Her cousin's argument made sense. But she could see her parents resorting to any measure to pay for the rehab—even selling the family house. "Rach, you know they'll do everything in their power to see that I'm in rehab."

"Don't you see? You're *already* in rehab. You have a doctor who's on top of the case. Harold's a great therapist. And the aqua sessions are going well, too. That's all you have to tell them."

Frowning, Sam wasn't so sure. "And the reason I'm back in Rosewood?"

"You came home." Rachel's face filled with affection. "Is there any better reason? And you don't have to do it by yourself." She leaned forward earnestly. "I'll be here. Mom and Dad, too. That way, you can hand the phone off to them, let my parents convince Aunt Joyce and Uncle Ed that you're okay…in good hands."

Nervously, Sam considered the idea. "What if—"

"If you consider all the contingencies, all the possible questions, you'll never tell them. Besides not worrying them, have you thought how hurt they'll be if they hear you're home from someone else? The Carrutherses have convinced all your neighbors to keep mum, but one of your parents' friends is bound to see you either at the hospital, or out riding in the car with one of us. What then?"

Indeed. What then? "You're right."

"Whew. I was hoping you'd see the light. I'll call my parents, see what time they can be over."

"Now?" Panic made her breathing shallow. Claustrophobia followed.

Rachel's voice gentled. "Sam, the longer you have to dwell on it, the harder it'll be. Besides, think how thrilled they'll be to hear you rode a horse!"

Since Uncle Don was retired, his schedule was open. Within the hour, Samantha was surrounded by her family.

Aunt Trudy hugged her, a fierce hug for such a small lady. "It'll be fine, honey. And we'll be right here."

"Not exactly *right* here, Mom." Rachel gave her mother a meaningful glance Sam couldn't fail to see. "While Sam gets them on the phone, we can have some iced tea in the dining room. And everyone remember the ground rules—no mention of the fire."

Rachel herded her parents into the dining room as Samantha clicked her phone on, then gripped the now crumpled paper with her parents' number. She had folded and unfolded the paper dozens of times since her cousin had called in the troops. Ground rules. Good idea, but Samantha was almost sure she was going to have a meltdown.

Taking a deep breath, she punched in the numbers. Hearing her father's voice, she felt the onset of tears. "Dad?"

"Punkin, that you?" Hearty cheer all the way from Africa made her pull the phone even closer.

"It's me."

"We were beginning to get worried. Haven't talked to you in longer than I can remember. I know our coverage is sketchy, so we probably missed some calls. We love your letters, but we need to hear your voice, Sam. When we've called, we've always gotten your voice mail. You okay?"

"Yes." Sam swallowed, feeling guilty about the subterfuge of having a friend in New York mail the letters so there wasn't a telltale Rosewood postmark. "There's nothing to worry about."

"Sam, I hate to let the cat out of the bag, but parents never stop worrying."

A single tear slipped down her cheek. "You've had way too much of that."

"Nope. Won't ever happen. You're stuck with us and we love you."

Another tear followed. "I love you, too, Dad."

"What's wrong?"

She sniffed quietly, then made herself get under control. "Actually, it's just the opposite. Something's right." She paused. "I'm back home…in Rosewood."

"Samantha! You're better?"

She thought of the tiny, barely measurable movement in her hips. "Yes."

"I'll talk to your mother, see when we can get a flight—"

"No!" She calmed her voice. "I mean, you don't need to. Uncle Don and Aunt Trudy are here. And Rachel. Of course, the Carrutherses are here almost nonstop. I have tons of help." She didn't dare mention Bret. Her parents would instantly know she wasn't completely coming clean.

"Semester break is just around the corner—"

She gripped the phone more tightly. "Actually, I was thinking about Thanksgiving. It'd really be special for us to be together then. We could celebrate with the whole family." And the kitchen should be nearing completion by then.

"You'll have to convince your mother." He spoke to Joyce, then the connection crackled as he handed the phone over.

"Sweetie, you there?" Her mother's worried voice came through as clearly as if she stood in the same room instead of continents away.

"Hi, Mom. I was just telling Dad that Uncle Don, Aunt Trudy and Rachel are here."

"That's good, but what about your rehab?"

"I'm going to therapy every day, Mom. It's a more aggressive program than I was in before. And J. C. Mueller is just as good as any of the doctors in New York." All true. Thank goodness. She could never lie to her parents.

"Oh. I hadn't thought of that. But your dad says you don't want us to come home."

"It's not that, Mom. I was kind of hoping we could celebrate Thanksgiving together…with the family. It's not that long from now." Sam bit down on her lower lip, hoping she sounded convincing. "Besides, it makes me feel better knowing you're helping Andy's kids."

"Oh, sweetie." Joyce's voice clogged with emotion.

Sam brushed away another tear. "The school means a lot to me, Mom."

"The school's important, but we want to be there for you, too."

"You always are." More tears collected and her voice warbled. "I don't know if I've ever told you how much that means to me."

Her mother's soft weeping traveled through the line. "Oh, Samantha. We love you so much."

"Me, too."

Don walked in to the living room, his steps quiet.

"Mom? Uncle Don wants to talk to you." Emotionally spent, Sam handed the phone to him.

Moments later, Rachel motioned for her to come into the dining room.

Leaving her uncle to finish the task, Samantha rolled up to the table.

"I listened," Rachel confided without remorse. "You did great."

Trudy leaned over and gave Sam another even fiercer hug, then headed toward the living room.

Rachel smiled encouragingly. "Your parents are going to be okay with this."

Sam's lips trembled. "I don't deserve them."

"Of course you do, numb-nut." Rachel then tsked under her breath. "Honestly, I've heard of emotional roller coasters, but you're close to being an entire amusement park." She tiptoed next to the arched opening that led into the living room so she could listen again.

Don's voice was quiet, but audible. "Ed, Sam's progressing well. Coming home now...well, she might regress if she feels responsible for you leaving the school."

Rachel glanced back. "Dad's doing a good job."

"I *can* still hear."

"Excuse me. Didn't know you'd become a bat." Rachel peeked around the corner. "Now Mom's taking the phone."

Although Trudy was more emotional, she did a good job of convincing them that Samantha was in good hands.

Rachel returned to the table and took a long sip of tea. "I keep telling you not to worry and I've got myself wound up in a knot. You'd think we're planning on overthrowing the government instead of getting you well."

Surprising herself, Samantha was amused at her cousin's lack of composure.

"Okay, what's funny?" Rachel demanded.

"You. Miss Cool and Calm. You're supposed to be supporting *me*, not turning into jelly."

"Make you a deal. Next time I'm trying to pull a fast one on my parents, I'll let you do all the worrying."

As though that would happen. Rachel was both close to and protective of Don and Trudy. Even though she and Rachel had occasionally gotten into mischief as kids, it had never been serious. They hadn't found anything to rebel against. Levelheaded and fair, both sets of parents had given them ideal childhoods.

Ones Samantha had only recently realized were so rare, so valuable.

She listened as her aunt and uncle finished the phone call, eager to hear her parents' side of the conversation.

"They're worried," Don admitted. "But any parent would be. I did my best to convince them that we'd be here for you."

"Thanks. I know this wasn't easy for you." Samantha hesitated, knowing the commitment she was about to make was one she couldn't renege on. "But I promise to put everything I've got into therapy…try whatever J.C. suggests."

Rachel whooped aloud. Trudy's eyes moistened and Don's face wreathed into lines of relief.

Seeing how much they cared, she was overwhelmed. Although she'd loved her globe-trotting, Samantha was beginning to realize how much she had missed being gone. This level of care…the special bonds she shared with her family.

A flash of Bret's thoughtfulness hit her. The care and trouble he'd taken to make the horseback riding experience happen. Closing her eyes, she couldn't stop wondering. By leaving, had she forever missed out on the one man she loved?

Chapter Eight

Bret grabbed an apple from a basket on the counter in his parents' kitchen.

"These muffins will be done in a few minutes," his mother, Nancy, offered.

"Don't have time." He glanced over at his father. "Besides, apple cinnamon's Dad's favorite."

Nancy met his gaze, her own touched with concern. "If he'll eat them."

"Dad pass up those?" Bret took the chair next to his father's. "No chance, huh?"

Robert reached for the newspaper. "Just a little tired today."

"You been to the doctor?"

"Now you sound like your mother." Robert opened the pages. "Nothing's wrong. I just spent more time outside than I planned on."

"And he didn't take his vitamins."

Robert looked fondly at his wife. "Snitch. It's that new calcium pill, upsets my stomach."

Years of practice made Nancy seem casual. "We'll tell the doctor next time."

Robert eyed his eldest. "She's already got a list as long as her arm. Poor man's going to go deaf with all those complaints—that, or wish he could."

Nancy swatted him playfully, but the worry never left her expression. "Bret, I've got a casserole dish of Janie's I keep forgetting to return. Would you mind taking it to work and giving it to Herb?"

"No problem. 'Course, he'd like it more if it was full of something you cooked."

"Janie's getting better." Nancy defended her youngest with a wryness none of them could miss. "Besides, cooking isn't everything. She has a lot of other talents."

Robert rustled the newspaper. "Not that'll fit in that casserole dish."

Bret took his cue. "Gotta run. Dad, you need any supplies?" He ordered their gardening accessories along with the nursery's.

"I'm good. Maybe next week."

Trying to look as encouraging as possible, Bret winked at his mother. "Don't let him get too rambunctious. I've got enough to wrangle at work."

She smiled, then rested her hand on Robert's shoulder. "I'll do my best."

With his father's health on his mind, Bret headed over to the nursery. He was surprised to see Peter's car in the lot along with Herb's truck. Actually on time. Needing a good sign, Bret decided to take it as one.

Since Herb's truck was unlocked, he put the casserole dish on the bench seat.

Before going inside, he checked on the youngest group of Christmas trees, pleased with their progress. It was just a matter of education and people would love them—and get as accustomed to them as a newly chopped tree.

Inside, Herb was at the counter, studying some papers while Peter watched from a nearby aisle.

Bret paused at a newly arranged display of baby squash and miniature pumpkins. Perfect for autumn. Must have been Herb's idea. Whistling, Bret glanced over the aisles leading to the counter. All were looking good.

Herb looked up as he approached. "Hey. Maybe you can help me figure out this report."

Bret was surprised. "You're the computer whiz."

"Not a computer problem. We're running low on the premium potting soil and I can't see where it's been ordered."

Considering that particular potting soil was one of their top sellers, it should have been flagged to order. "Maybe you've got an old list."

"Don't think so. Just ran the report today. Couldn't find the topsoil on it, so I printed out the last several orders. No topsoil ordered, regular or premium."

Bret gritted his teeth, then forced himself to unclench his jaw. "Peter?"

"Playing up to the boss, Herbie?" Peter thumped his

head. "That's right. You don't need to. You've got the job all sewn up."

Bret and Peter had shared the ordering tasks, so Bret couldn't automatically blame his employee. "Why didn't you tell me we were running low?"

Peter shrugged. "I'm supposed to be the outside guy, remember?"

"You're supposed to be working both sides, *remember*?"

"Yeah, like that's gonna matter. Right, Herbie?"

Brow scrunched upward, Herb looked everywhere but at Peter. Deciding his brother-in-law had the right idea, Bret went into the office. He pulled out the probation file on Peter. It was the first one he had ever been forced to make. Conway's was a family business in the truest sense. And Bret didn't like the idea of firing an employee. Since the nursery had been established, everyone who worked there had been treated well and they'd reciprocated by working as though the business was their own.

But labor laws had changed over the years. And with the nursery on precarious financial ground, he didn't dare allow any loose threads that could lead to litigation. If he didn't document Peter's behavior, the man could take his case to the labor commission, meaning expensive lawyers. But Bret didn't see any outcome other than termination.

Herb stuck his head through the open doorway. "What about the soil?"

"I'll call the vendor, put it on a rush. Then I need

to get you up to speed on inventory and ordering. Should have already done it. With the holidays coming, we can't afford to lose any regular trade."

Herb's expression was wryly sympathetic. "I'm rethinking the benefits of owning your own business. You can't get laid off, but I didn't know you had to worry about mutiny."

"He's the exception."

"You're taking on a lot, Bret. Running this place, watching out for your parents, doing for Samantha. Can I help?"

"You already are. We both know what's going to happen with Peter. Frankly, I'll be glad when his ninety days are up."

"What about Sam's kitchen? Need another volunteer?"

"Couldn't hurt. I've pulled in quite a few people, but there's a lot of work."

"Count me in."

Bret was restless. And he couldn't get Sam out of his thoughts. Worried about his father and the business, he'd been busy the last several weeks. He'd had to hand off several of Sam's therapy sessions to Rachel. And breakfasts had been hurried, sometimes just dropping hers by.

Strangely, it wasn't guilt or duty he was feeling. It was something more. Something that made him dwell on the deep azure-blue of her eyes, the soft curve of her cheek.

Refusing to analyze the reasons, he quickly punched in Sam's phone number. She answered on the third ring.

"Thought you might like to get out—go to the park."

"Oh." Her voice faltered for a moment. "Aren't you busy?"

"Truth? Yeah. But I could use the break." And he could justify the time because Conway's had the landscape contract for the park. Not that the park needed checking, but he could justify it. Refusing to question the foolishness of leaving work in the middle of the day, Bret drove to Sam's.

She waited on the porch, her expression cautious, questioning. "I'm surprised you're playing hooky from work."

"Best part of being the boss." He grasped the handles and pushed her to the Blazer. Picking her up, he realized his memory of how soft she felt against him was completely accurate. Completely unnerving. Although he wanted to linger, he got her settled, then stowed the wheelchair in back.

The park was at its best on the clear, early autumn day. Leafy trees in transition still held their glorious, changing colors. A few mothers played with their young children while old men sat on benches, feeding birds and passing the time.

"I'd forgotten how pretty our park is," Sam murmured as Bret pushed her chair toward the center fountain. "How soothing the water is." She continued to stare at the flow of the water. "You won't believe what I did."

He waited.

"Called my parents, told them I'm here."

Surprised, Bret stared at her. "What brought that on?"

"About time, don't you think?"

Bret remained silent.

"Realized I was being selfish," Sam continued, "expecting everyone else to do the worrying, keeping my secret."

For a few minutes only the sound of water resonated between them. A blue jay shrieked as it flew at a smaller bird, startling a covey of sparrows, which then erupted from a nearby oak tree.

"They're reacting the way you're trying not to," Samantha said in a quiet voice.

"I'll admit I'm surprised."

"Shocked and disbelieving." She lifted her face and the midday sun bathed her creamy skin. Since she'd regained a small bit of the weight she'd lost, her delicate features were re-blossoming. She was as lovely as she'd been in college. Only the residual pain in her deep-blue eyes had changed her. But that only made her more appealing.

Bret pulled a penny from his pocket, then tossed it in the fountain. "Make a wish."

She exhaled, a mocking sound.

"Or pray for what you want."

"Not something I do anymore."

Her faith had always been deep, secure. "Maybe you need to start."

"So I can lose someone again?"

Andy.

Bret took the handles of her chair, leaving the sidewalk to walk on the soft grass. It was a little bumpy as he took them down the path to the glorious old magnolia tree that was the centerpiece of the park.

Concentrating on his footing, he didn't look up until they were a few feet from the tree. He stopped abruptly, staring. The normally glossy, vibrant green leaves were brown, some of the thick branches nearly bare.

"Oh no!" Reaching upward, Sam made a move as though to get up from the chair. Her legs didn't cooperate and she slumped back. "*Magnolia grandiflora,*" she murmured.

Most people called it the southern magnolia—a tree of grand and gorgeous proportions. And this one had been thriving in the park since long before they were born. Now, it looked as though the ninety-foot-tall magnolia might perish.

Although still unable to reach it, Samantha stretched out toward the tree, her face wreathed in concern. "Do you know what's wrong?"

"It's been fine." He shook his head, unable to imagine what had happened to the magnolia. "We had a long drought cycle, but the last few years have been better."

"It wouldn't just now be suffering from a drought

that long ago." She craned her neck, looking upward. "Has it been overwatered to make up for the dryness?"

"No. We have the contract for maintaining the park. And you know Mac. He's been the caretaker most of his life—he knows his stuff." Mac, a city employee, mowed, edged and weeded, but Conway's was responsible for landscaping and maintaining the trees and plants.

Sam wheeled backward a few feet for a broader view. "Roots aren't above ground."

"I covered them with soil in the spring, enough to keep in the moisture, not enough to keep the water from draining."

"Were there any nicks or cuts on the exposed roots from the riding lawn mower?" she questioned, rolling back up toward the trunk.

"Nope. Mac doesn't use the mower near the roots."

She narrowed her eyes, studying the tree. "Do you have a pocket knife?"

He pulled it out.

"Can you make a small cut in the bark?"

Complying, he handed her the newly incised bark.

"Bret, is the trunk green beneath the cut?"

"Barely."

"But not brown?"

He shook his head.

"Good. It's still alive."

"Do you think you can save it?"

Startled, she stared at him. "Me?"

"Conway's reputation is on the line. I'm a horticulturist, not a plant pathologist."

"Magnolias don't heal well. A specimen, even this old, can die just from under- or overwatering."

"But you're the expert."

"I'm not a miracle worker!" The words barely out of Samantha's mouth, the color drained from her face.

"So you're not up to it?" He knelt next to the base of the tree, unable to believe the stalwart magnolia was in such bad condition.

Sam visibly swallowed. "You can't get to me like that."

"Like what? You've been all over the world diagnosing diseased plants and now you don't think you can handle one tree in your hometown?"

A glimmer of fire simmered in her eyes. "It's not that simple and you know it."

Getting up, he dusted off his knees, looking around for Mac. The older man was usually easy to find. But Bret couldn't see him.

Sam didn't seem to notice. "That tree doesn't have any more hope than I do!"

Her words drew his gaze back immediately. "The magnolia doesn't have any choice, it has to be tended by someone else."

Samantha trembled with indignation. "And you think I have a choice?"

"Every day. Whether you really try with your therapy and keep your thoughts positive, or whether you're going to just give up—"

"You don't know everything!" she burst out.

He gently rocked on his heels. "I hope not. All that knowledge—my head might explode."

Clearly exasperated, she huffed. "I already promised my family I would put everything I have into the therapy."

Surprised, Bret didn't reply.

"I said you didn't know everything," Sam muttered.

"Apparently not."

"If, *if* I agree to run some tests on the tree, you have to back off. And I'm not promising anything."

Back off. Considering how she was drawing him in again, making him need her in his life…all round, it was probably best for both of them.

"No, Mom," Sam insisted, holding her cell phone with one hand while trying to roll her wheelchair with the other. "I'm not doing too much. J.C. said I need a more intensive therapy routine. Right now I'm doing both the water classes and physical therapy."

"All right, sweetheart. I'm so glad you're close to the family. Helps, doesn't it?"

Samantha glanced over at Rachel, who waited across the room for the call to end. "It really does."

"We love you."

Sam felt a fleeting desire to pray that her parents wouldn't be hurt if she didn't improve. Ignoring it, she swallowed. "Yeah. Me, too."

Clicking off, she stared at the phone before slowly replacing it in her pocket.

"Everything okay?" Rachel asked.

Samantha nodded. "She was just checking on me."

Rachel's forehead furrowed. "Sam?"

"I don't want them to be disappointed if my therapy doesn't work." She glanced at her cousin. "Despite what anyone thinks, I *am* trying."

Rachel frowned. "Who thinks you're not?"

"Bret, of course." Samantha couldn't keep the disappointed anger from her voice.

"Of course?" Rachel whistled. "Might want to give the guy a break. If it wasn't for him, I wouldn't even know you're home. Not to mention, he saved your bacon during the fire."

Sam grimaced at the pun.

Rachel studied her face. "So why do you think he's doubting your determination?"

"Because I said I couldn't help the dying magnolia in the park."

"I know the one you mean." Rachel leaned forward. "I can hardly believe what shape it's in. Almost overnight, too." She frowned. "It's what you do. Why can't you fix it?"

If only life were that simple. "I can't *fix it* any more than I can fix my legs. I could run some tests, but a lot of times, magnolias don't heal from something as routine as pruning. This one practically needs a rebirth."

"It's dead?"

Sam hesitated. "Not yet. But—"

"Then why are you procrastinating? I'm sure Bret's done all he can. It's up to you."

Why couldn't anyone understand? "I'm not a miracle worker."

"I wish you could hear yourself! Samantha Shaw doesn't give up." Exasperated, Rachel rose and paced the floor between them. "You promised Dad you'd try, *really* try. If you don't believe you can succeed, well, what are you trying to do? Fool everyone?"

Silenced, Sam put her hands together, interlacing her fingers over and over again.

Abruptly Rachel thumped down into a chair. "Sorry."

"I *am* trying. I wasn't lying to your dad. I just don't share everyone's…optimism."

"What aren't you telling me?"

Sam thought of the family connections she'd let go rusty, and the man she'd undervalued and lost. "It's a lot of change, Rach. Not just the chair. Coming back here. Knowing I can't have the same kind of career." She held up her hand to keep Rachel from interrupting. "Even if the therapy helps somehow, I won't be able to trudge through forests, climb mountains. You're not the only one who talks to J.C. I'll still have spinal damage. Probably sounds selfish, but I don't understand why this had to happen. I've told myself a zillion times that other people have bad things happen, too. Worse things. But I thought we had our allotment when we lost Andy."

"Yeah."

Sam looked out the window at the charming, brick-paved street. "Maybe it was growing up here. Feeling safe. Almost invincible." That time seemed so long ago. When she'd run home from school every day to the comforting sounds and smells of home, the welcoming arms of her family.

Rachel sighed.

When Rachel didn't have a heartening suggestion, there wasn't one. Not wanting to see her cousin so down, Samantha dredged up a smile. "Maybe everyone looks back on their childhood through rose-colored glasses. I suppose I need to be looking forward instead."

Rachel's face eased into a hopeful smile. "Sam! You mean that?"

She nodded, unwilling to let the wobble she felt in her throat spill out. But Rachel didn't hold back, sniffling as she brushed her own tears away.

"Oh, Rach!" Hating that she'd upset her cousin, Samantha reached out.

Rachel's hug was fierce. "I've been so afraid that you'd give up, that we'd lose you."

Samantha felt the wetness of Rachel's tears against her shoulder. Guilt from the pain she was causing her family swamped her. She'd been so blind…so caught up in only herself.

What, Samantha wondered, would it take to move beyond that inner concern? Again she thought of Bret.

To find a way to heal the relationships she had damaged….

Bret lifted a pile of charred wood from the back porch of Sam's house. He'd brought his old pickup truck to load up the debris. He planned to recycle it into ash for planting beds.

Fortunately, the kitchen was coming along. He and Matt had asked another friend, Seth McAllister, to redraw the design plans to incorporate the upgrades Joyce wanted. With Seth's guidance, they were making other changes that would improve the overall layout.

Bret shifted more pieces of the wood. Despite the other volunteers, there was still plenty of wreckage to be hauled away.

The noise must have alerted Sam, because she was out on the porch when he walked up the driveway. He'd left a thermos of coffee on the front steps, planning to get the truck loaded before Sam woke. Her hair was tousled, her face dewy with sleep. Eyes quiescent, guileless, she smiled. Instantly, he vaulted a decade back in time. Then their smiles had been unguarded, filled with love. No shadows, no regret.

The push-pull of his emotions was as confusing as the attraction that kept building, the need to be close to Sam. Wishing he had an off switch for his feelings, Bret dumped the load into his truck.

As he did, she rolled down the ramp toward him. "Old Red," she murmured, touching one rounded truck fender.

It was the fond nickname they'd had for the battered old truck he'd driven all through high school and college—a gift from his grandfather. "It's a stubborn thing." Bret pulled off his work gloves and ran one hand over the edge of the truck's roof. "Won't say die."

"Lot of good times in that truck." Her voice was soft, filled with nostalgia.

"Yeah."

Sam blinked, seeming to come back to the present. "How about some coffee? I saw your thermos."

He glanced toward the backyard where more debris waited.

"Mrs. Carruthers brought over fresh kolaches," she tempted.

His stomach rumbled. Kolaches, a Czech pastry filled with anything from fruit to sausage, were a local breakfast treat. And difficult to refuse. Following her up the ramp, Bret grabbed the coffee, then settled into a rocker on one side of the small table.

As he poured coffee into the mugs Sam had brought out, she offered the plate of kolaches. "She made raspberry."

He took one. "One of my favorites."

"I know."

It was early enough in the morning that the birds were still chattering to one another in the trees, and squirrels collected newly fallen acorns.

Sam swallowed a bite of her kolache. "Rachel thinks you're right. That I should help the magnolia."

Surprised, he put his mug down. "And what do you think?"

Sam didn't meet his eyes. "I can try."

"No one can ask for more than that."

She lifted her gaze. "I'll need help, of course."

Bret knew how difficult it was for Sam to swallow her pride, to ask for assistance. Especially after she'd told him to back off. "You be the expert, I'll be the drudge." He gestured toward her unfinished kolache. "Eat your breakfast."

She took another bite, the raspberry filling reddening her full lips, then trickling a tiny way from her mouth.

Impulsively, Bret leaned over, wiping the sweet trace away with one thumb.

Their faces close, she looked into his eyes, seeming to search deep within his soul. The years melted away. They were back walking hand in hand, their future outstretched like a golden road. His gaze dropped to her lips, his fingers cupping her chin. Refusing to consider the consequences, he drew even closer, touching his lips to hers.

Her lips were as sweet as he remembered. Soft, gentle, beguiling.

He cradled the back of her head, twining his fingers in her silky hair, bringing her cheek next to his. As she tilted her head back, he lost himself in her eyes.

Chapter Nine

The blast of a horn split the morning air, causing Bret and Samantha to jerk backward. Nearly as quickly, Bret jumped up from the rocker and Sam blushed fiercely.

Matt Whitaker pulled into the driveway, then hopped out of his truck. "Morning. Need to get a few measurements. Saw Bret's truck, figured it wasn't too early…" The tension on the porch was so palpable Matt paused, then cleared his throat. "I can do that anytime. Need to get over to the shop."

Bret stepped forward, quickly swiping one hand over his mouth. "Let's head back to the kitchen. I've been clearing some of the mess. Good thing the rear door's solid. Fire would have eaten up the back of the house, too."

Matt caught Samantha's eye and nodded to her before following Bret inside.

They got as far as the entrance to the kitchen. Bret stopped short.

"What was that?" Matt asked, jerking his thumb in the direction of the porch.

Bret shrugged. "One minute…" He thumped his head. "I don't know."

"No one'd be happier to see you two get back together, but if it's not for keeps…"

"Never has been with us." Sighing, Bret tilted his head back, staring at the ceiling. "Don't know what I was thinking."

"She's had an awful lot happen to her these last few years. Losing Andy…that…" Matt cleared his throat. "Now, this accident. I'm wondering how she'll fare if you get back together and it doesn't work out."

"That's not going to happen," Bret decided as he spoke, trying to erase the memory of their kiss. "Wouldn't be good for either of us." Not when her idea of commitment was bailing when things got tough.

Matt thumped Bret's shoulder in understanding. "Better get that kitchen measured."

Bret realized he had to stop with the mixed signals. Now. No matter how sweet the kiss.

Itching to be gone from the scene of embarrassment, Samantha did something she hadn't done since coming back to Rosewood. She rolled down the porch and onto the sidewalk. By herself.

It was a strange feeling. From her seated position, Samantha viewed the street she'd grown up on at the same level she had as a child. There was the stone arch in the Carters' front yard that she'd once imagined was a drawbridge. There'd been no dragons, though.

And the stepping stones a few doors down that she'd struggled to leapfrog. The excitement she'd felt once she had grown tall enough to conquer them. Resisting self-pity, she smiled at the childhood triumph.

Trees seemed acres taller, as did everything. They, too, had grown along with the children of the neighborhood. Now a new generation of children played amongst the aged trees and thicketed gardens.

Sam knew she wasn't old. At least she'd never felt old before. Thirty. An age when many women were already married, raising children. She slowed to a near stop. She'd always thought there would be time for that. Later.

Had later passed her by? Had she really expected someone as fine as Bret to suddenly appear once she'd satisfied her thirst for discovery, adventure? Certainly wasn't going to be Bret himself. Especially since one kiss had made him flee for his life.

Samantha glanced at the grass. Even it seemed taller from her diminished perspective. The thought barely complete, she saw something move in the dense blades. A tiny head popped up. An equally tiny meow followed when the little thing opened its pink mouth.

"Oh my!" Samantha watched the kitten determinedly plow through what must have seemed like a massive field to such a small creature. Impulsively she leaned forward. "Kitty…here, kitty."

Baby button eyes fixed on her in surprise. Then, to Sam's delight, the kitten scampered her way.

"Well, hello." Sam held out her hand. "Who do you belong to?"

The kitten delicately examined her hand and Sam saw no collar. Probably had wandered away from the house she'd stopped in front of. Unable to resist, Sam picked up the animal, cradling it in her lap.

Unafraid, the miniature cat batted at her sleeve.

Light gray with white paws, the kitten was a cutie. "I guess we'd better get you back home."

The kitten was content to ride along as Sam wheeled up the sidewalk. At the steps she stopped, realizing she couldn't ring the bell.

As she wondered what to do, a woman pushed open the screen door. "Is that you, Sam?"

"Maddie?" They'd gone to school together. "I didn't know you still lived here."

"Not still. Back. Taking care of my mother."

"Oh, I'm sorry. I didn't know she was sick."

Maddie nodded. "She's had several strokes and they caused dementia. She can't live alone."

Sam remembered that Maddie's father had passed away when they were in high school.

"I heard you had an accident," Maddie continued. "I should have come over. It's just so hard to leave Mom alone."

"That's okay. You've got your hands full."

Maddie tilted her head toward the kitten. "You, too."

"Oh!" Sam smiled. "That's why I'm here. Is he yours?"

"No. I haven't seen him before. Doesn't look like he has a collar, either."

"I noticed. I guess I could ask the neighbors." Sam looked back toward the other houses with their daunting entrances.

"Why don't I call around?" Maddie offered. "There's a ramp on the side of the house. It's how I get Mom around. Why don't you come in? We'll see what we can find out."

"Well…okay. Sure. Why not?" Now adept with her wheelchair, Sam pivoted on the wide sidewalk and rolled down the driveway. The kitten was content to hang onto her sleeve.

Maddie met her at the back door. "Gosh, it's good to have company. I mean someone for me. I'm grateful people are faithful about visiting Mom. But, you know…" Maddie shrugged. "It's hard for friends of mine. They have their families to take care of. You know."

"I do."

"Yes…well." Maddie firmed her lips in instant understanding. "Let's start calling." She grabbed the slim Rosewood directory from the kitchen desk. "I just made some fresh tea. Would you like some? Or I could make coffee."

Sam didn't want any more coffee. "Tea sounds good."

Maddie took two delicate china cups and saucers from the cabinet. "I used to think it was silly that Mom used these for everyday when they have to be washed by hand. She said it made the tea more special. Funny. Now I think she's right."

"I've been rediscovering a lot lately myself. Learning I appreciated way too little."

Maddie carefully placed the cups on the table. An equally delicate sugar bowl and creamer were already on the round oak table. "Do you take lemon?"

"No, thanks." Sam lifted the cup. "It smells heavenly."

"Probably the hibiscus in the blend."

"I didn't know we had a store here that sells fancy teas."

Maddie smiled. "We don't. I make this myself."

"Wow." Sam sipped a bit of the tea. "It's really good."

"I'm glad you like it. I've always wanted to open a little speciality tea shop. Make and sell the blends, have a few tables so I could serve customers, maybe carry some pastries."

"Why don't you?"

Maddie's smile was at odds with the sadness in her eyes. "Mom. She needs me."

"Oh."

"A lot of my friends tell me I should put her in a home. But she's always been there for me, you know? Now it's my turn."

"Has she been sick long?"

"About seven years."

Sam thought of all the freedom she'd had. Freedom she'd never given a second thought. "She's very lucky to have you."

"You probably won't believe me, but I feel the same

about her. My only regret is the time I was away at college. Turns out those were the last years before her first stroke. What I miss most is our talks. Sounds cliché, but she really is my best friend. And I miss her advice. I still find myself wanting to turn to her when I have a problem, even when it's her care that's the problem."

For the first time since her accident, Sam saw someone who had sacrificed more. Unconsciously, she stroked the kitten's back, comforted by the soft, furry body.

"I guess I'd better start making those calls." Maddie flipped open the directory. "Let's start next door. They have two little boys. Maybe little kittens, too?"

"So you haven't seen her?" Bret forced himself to remain calm, to sound calm. "I'm sure she's fine, Rachel. Don't worry your parents. Obviously Sam can't have gone far. I'll call as soon as I find her." His face dropped into grim lines as soon as he clicked off his cell.

He had searched the house, even places Sam's wheelchair couldn't have possibly reached. Then he'd driven all over the neighborhood, going as far as Main Street. Alerting J.C., he'd had the hospital searched as well. Now, walking the streets of Sam's neighborhood, Bret was a step from panic.

She'd been missing longer than he could rationalize anymore. When he couldn't find her for lunch, he thought she must be with Rachel. He checked his watch. Nearly four o'clock. If she'd been gone since breakfast, that meant eight hours. Eight hours alone, unable to leave her wheelchair unassisted. Wishing he didn't have to, Bret dialed the sheriff's office. Tucker Gray answered.

"Glad it's you, Tuck." Bret quickly outlined what he knew. "This is the third time I've searched this block—all sides of it."

"I'll send out my deputies. Can you get together a list of any places she might go or people she might contact?"

"It'll be a short list, Tuck. I've already been by her aunt and uncle's house. Rachel hasn't seen her."

"Let's start a neighbor contact. I'm on my way."

Bret had already checked with the closest neighbors. "Right."

Running, he passed those houses, then loped to the next one. As he did, Bret saw something glint through the hedge in the late afternoon sun. "Samantha?" Realizing he'd only whispered, Bret raised his voice. "Samantha!"

The glint moved through the bushes as he ran toward them. She surfaced at the break between the driveway and the next house.

"Sam!"

Startled, she jerked toward him.

Panting, he stopped inches from her chair. "Where have you been?"

"I—"

"You've got half the town on alert. The sheriff's on his way—"

"The *sheriff*?" Her mouth fell open.

Remembering Tucker, Bret grabbed his cell phone,

dialing rapidly. "I found her. No. She's all right. Thank you." He glared at Sam, furious that she looked so calm. "What were you thinking?"

"Quit hollering. You're scaring the kitten."

Confused, he finally focused on the small bundle of fluff in her lap. "What are you doing with *that*?"

"*That* is a kitten. And she's lost."

"You've been out searching all day for a lost cat?" Vaulting from near terror to exasperation zapped the remainder of his waning patience.

"Hardly. I found her this morning."

Bret counted silently to ten. "And since then?"

She drew back, some of the old Samantha spirit igniting her eyes. "I don't report to you."

He felt his nostrils flare with indignation. Especially since he had a full day's worry bottled inside. "You might do me the courtesy of letting me know you haven't been kidnapped while I'm working on your house."

Her eyes transformed, softening in realization. "I didn't mean to worry you. I just needed to…get away."

Bret didn't want to know where Sam had chosen to escape. The reminder of why she'd left was too fresh…too raw. "As long as you're all right, no harm done." He wasn't sure why he was covering up how he really felt. Or how the anger had melted into something he didn't want to acknowledge. It was more than one kiss, more than the increasing attraction he felt for her.

No, the hold of her gaze convinced him he'd been reckless with his heart. And he wasn't sure any longer how to stop it.

Chapter Ten

"She's a cute little thing," Rachel cooed as she tried to coax the kitten to play with her. "I've never seen a kitten stick to a person like she does to you."

"Tabby jumps down when she wants, but when I go from room to room, she follows."

"Tabby, huh? I thought you weren't going to name her."

"I couldn't just call her Cat. Too *Breakfast at Tiffany's* for me. I'm not the Bohemian sort."

"Really?" Rachel muttered, storing some cat food on a low shelf where Samantha could reach it.

"I'm not!" Sam protested.

"What would you call trotting around the globe?"

"Being a *scientist*. Honestly, Rachel. The rest of the world isn't Rosewood. Then again, Rosewood isn't the rest of the world."

"Going to be a philosopher next?"

"Actually, I thought I might be a plant pathologist.

I'm going today with Bret to check the progress on the magnolia. He's dug drainage channels around the base of its trunk."

Delighted, Rachel jumped up. "Whoo hoo!"

Tabby stared at the unexpected hubbub while Samantha laughed at her cousin's mercurial mood change. "It's a drainage trench, not the English Channel."

"It's progress!" Rachel scooped up the flyers with Tabby's photo. She'd already located a hammer, which was stowed in her purse. "I'll get these tacked up around the neighborhood. If you're lucky, no one will claim her."

"I don't want to keep Tabby from her owner." Samantha stroked the kitten's back solicitously.

Rachel rolled her eyes. "Of course you don't. Want me to post the flyers behind trees and under bushes?"

"Okay. So I like her. A lot. But I want to do the right thing. I'd hate to think there's a child somewhere crying its eyes out over losing a pet."

"You're an impossible softie. But the little thing must be way off course. All the neighbors have been contacted and no one knows anything about her." Rachel shrugged. "Face it. She could be a stray."

Samantha was growing more attached to little Tabby every day. "I called the sheriff. He said he didn't have a missing report on her."

Bret's familiar knock sounded on the door. Rachel opened it with a smile. "Just on my way to alert the world about Sam's little find."

"She's probably a stray," Bret replied, holding the door for Rachel as she scooted past.

"Tell her that."

"She's probably a stray," Bret repeated for Samantha's benefit.

"Do you think I ought to get a little tag with my phone number in case Tabby gets out? I still want to find her owner, but I wouldn't want her to get lost again."

"We can stop at the pet store after the park. Going to have to get a collar to hang that tag on."

The magnolia didn't look any different, other than the low, sloping channels surrounding it. Which was neither bad nor good. The slow-healing species wouldn't show any visible progress for some time. And the channels had only been dug a week before.

Bret scooped up a handful of soil and gave it to Samantha.

She let it sift between her fingers. "Not too wet."

"We haven't had a good rain since I trenched it."

"I'll still need to take a sample, get it analyzed." She pulled a plastic, zippered bag from the fanny pack at her waist and handed it to Bret. "Soil could be nutrient-deficient."

"Have you heard anything on the tree bark sample we took the first day?" he asked.

Samantha shook her head. "Not yet, but I want to rule out the chance of wood borers."

Kneeling, Bret gathered a substantial amount of soil, then held up the bag. "This enough?"

"Could you get some of the bark mulch that's mixed in with the soil around the perimeter? I want to send the lab everything we can so they'll be able to run additional tests if the first ones don't give us an answer."

"It's a good start, Sam." He glanced up at the aging tree. "I'd sure hate to lose this old guy."

"It might not make it through the winter," she cautioned. Like herself, the tree had no real chance. Not the chance everyone was hoping for.

"You'll see, come spring. There's always hope." He handed her the sack, their hands grazing, lingering. "Always."

The memory of their shared kiss sprung to mind. And though Samantha couldn't be sure, she believed Bret was thinking about it, too. Remembering? Or regretting?

The pet shop wasn't busy. Two people were looking at the fish and a little boy kept trying to stick his hand into a parrot's cage.

"What kind of collar?" Bret asked, standing by the display.

"Pink. Not just 'cause she's a girl, but because it'll look good with her gray fur. Pale pink though, not that neon one."

He dug through until he found one small enough. They'd already learned that a permanent ID tag had to be ordered, but Sam picked out one to use in the interim that could be written on with a laundry marker, then encased in plastic.

"I don't suppose I really need to order a permanent tag," Sam murmured.

"Doesn't cost much." Bret was fairly certain the kitten wouldn't be claimed. And it was apparent Sam was already attached to the tiny animal. "Which shape do you like?"

"The heart." Sam decided instantly as she looked up at the illustrated display.

Bret filled out the order form and added it to their purchases. Rachel had brought over the essentials—food and a litter tray. Now, Sam took her time choosing toys she thought Tabby would enjoy.

Bemused by Sam's uncharacteristic behavior, Bret tried not to think about the time and how he should be back at work. Collecting the bags, he pushed her wheelchair outside to the Blazer. Just as he lifted her inside, his cell rang. Once she was safely settled, he answered.

"Bret? It's Rachel. I'm supposed to take Sam for her appointment with J.C. and then to therapy, but I took so much time putting up the posters that I have to get back to work. Since it's Friday, we have staff meeting and I can't miss it."

Bret glanced at his watch. Herb was at the nursery for the whole day and he could delay checking on his dad until later. "I can do it."

"You're a lifesaver."

He slid into his own side. "Looks like you're stuck with me."

She glanced at his cell. "Rachel?"

"Yep." He started the car, glancing into the rearview mirror before pulling out on to the street. "You didn't tell me you have an appointment with J.C."

"I thought I'd see how it goes."

She looked so nervous, Bret decided to give her a break. After phoning Herb to let him know the new plans, Bret was quiet as they drove to the doctor's, then got situated in an exam room.

J.C. soon followed. The chart he held was thicker than when Bret had last seen it.

"I've been studying your case files," J.C. began after the pleasantries. "Took longer than I expected to get everything from New York. But I got the last records a few days ago. I'm pleased to say your prognosis isn't nearly as grim as you predicted."

Bret straightened in his chair, listening intently.

"As I told you before, yours is an incomplete injury," J.C. continued.

"Incomplete?" Bret questioned.

"Means she's only partially paralyzed and could regain most of her mobility."

"That's great!" Realizing he'd raised his voice, Bret quieted, turning to Sam. "Don't you think so?"

She looked torn. "I'm afraid to raise everyone's hopes."

Especially her own.

J.C. flipped through the pages. "Your doctors immediately gave you a powerful corticosteroid that helps prevent further damage after the injury."

He turned several more pages. "On the home front,

I'm pleased with the results of your electrode therapy. Steady progress on muscle contraction."

Bret wished he knew more about all this terminology. "What's that?"

"We stimulate intact peripheral nerves with electrodes attached to the skin—causes the muscles to contract." J.C. turned to Samantha. "The movement in your hips isn't as insignificant as you thought. It means your muscles are responding." He flipped another page. "I'm impressed by the amount of time you've spent on the supported stander."

Bret looked at J.C.

"It's a device that supports the majority of Sam's weight as she exercises. It provides reciprocal movement of the arms and legs. It's in preparation for walking on her own, using only a bar to hold on to."

"And?" Sam looked as though she was hanging on to the last thread of her shredded nerves.

"There's no *and*," J.C. replied. "Sorry to disappoint you, but I don't have another shoe to drop. I want you to continue with your aqua and physical therapy."

"That's really it?" she asked.

Bret could see she was torn between relief and fear.

J.C. scrunched his forehead in thought. "Well, actually…"

Sam leaned forward, her expression feverish, obviously dreading the worst.

He glanced at the chart. "According to this, you begin work on the parallel bars today. So I expect you to go for the gold."

It took Samantha a moment to realize he was gently teasing. Then she exhaled.

"Sam, I'm not holding anything back. Your records have only confirmed what I've thought from the start. Your immediate trauma care was excellent. So was your surgery. You already know that your muscles atrophied from the length of your coma, and it takes a lot of therapy to reverse that effect. You've shown great progress so far—your leg muscles are responding." J.C. leaned forward. "When you start on the parallel bars today, you need to believe the therapy will work."

For once, Samantha seemed at a loss for words.

"Sam's determined," Bret answered for her. "She already promised the family she'll do her best."

The physical therapy section was fairly quiet: only a few patients were being treated.

However, Sam's nerves were so tight she felt as though she might implode at any moment. "We could do this another time…when Rachel doesn't have to work."

"I'll try not to bite until we're done."

She clasped her hands together, threading her long, slender fingers together over and over again. "Everybody's counting on me to do well."

"So do well." Bret glanced around at the other equipment.

She thumped her forehead. "Silly me. I should have thought of that."

"That's what you've got me for."

Harold waved from the opposite side of the room. It was do or die time.

Since Samantha had already confided her fears about the parallel bars, Harold took it slow as he eased her from the wheelchair.

"Remember, you did well on the supported standers," Harold encouraged. For Bret's benefit, he pointed to a machine on the adjacent wall. "That one's designed to transition from sitting to standing. The straps keep the user fully supported, so it's like standing, but with help."

Which she wouldn't have on the parallel bars. Sam felt a trickle of sweat slip down her neck, then travel over her chest. She gripped the parallel bars, her hands slippery as well. Despite the therapist's encouragement, she was terrified to leave the safety of her wheelchair.

Bret stood at the opposite end of the parallel bars as though he expected her to just stroll into his arms. The distance looked like miles instead of yards.

Harold remained upbeat. "You're doing great."

Considering she hadn't moved a solitary inch, that wasn't even close to being true.

"Did I tell you I'm in charge of decorating Main Street for the holidays?" Bret asked out of the blue.

"Holidays?" Distracted, she jerked her attention from the task at hand.

"And I'll need help with them. I'd like to work up some new designs."

Sam stared at him. "I'm kind of busy here."

Bret shrugged. "It's not like you're running the Boston Marathon."

Fire ignited her blood. "And you know *so* much about it?" She lifted one foot. "I'd like to see you try this."

"Funny, I'd like to see *you* do it."

Gripping the bars more tightly, she tried the other foot. Therapy had strengthened her thighs and she squeezed them tightly, finally making her second foot move.

Bret still lounged at the end of the parallel bars, but his attention seemed more focused somehow. Then he mouthed the words: Do well.

"I am!" she replied aloud.

"I know," he responded, his expression warmer than she'd seen it in years.

Disconcerted, she glanced over at Harold, who looked equally pleased.

Then it hit her. She'd moved. Granted, only inches. But they were inches under her own power. "I…"

"Walked," Bret finished quietly.

"Walked," she repeated. Shaking with excitement, Samantha's eyes burned. She didn't dare release a hand from the bar to wipe away the spurt of tears.

Bret was at her side in seconds, easing them away with a lingering touch. "Can't have them blocking your view." His voice was husky, his eyes dark with emotion.

Samantha was so clogged with feeling she could only hold his gaze.

"All right, no goofing off." Bret placed one hand over hers, squeezing it gently.

Finding her voice, she agreed. "Right." She was at once exhilarated and overwhelmed. And determined to do it again. But the muscles in her upper thighs burned and her legs quivered as though she'd run miles. Taking a deep breath, she tried to lift one foot. Pain shot through her back with the effort.

"That's enough for today," Harold cautioned.

Samantha wanted to disagree, but absurdly, she was exhausted.

"Only aqua therapy tomorrow," Harold continued. "It vasodilates the vessels—increases the blood flow to your spine without pressure. We don't want to take things too quickly."

Sam swallowed another weepy spurt of emotion. Bret had egged her on, taunted, dared, distracted. And forced her to walk. Yet there wasn't a single *I told you so* in his expression. If anything, he looked as victorious as she felt. Was it possible…? Could there be just a fraction of his feeling left for her?

Chapter Eleven

Leaves, transformed by the coolness of autumn, crowded some tree branches, while others drifted to the ground, forming tempting piles. Children leapt into the deepest mounds while their dogs chased them, scattering even more leaves. It was a beautiful Saturday.

Samantha laughed at the antics as she rolled down the sidewalk toward Maddie's house. Despite taking two steps the day before, she wasn't ready to ditch the wheelchair yet.

This time she'd dutifully left a note for Bret so he wouldn't panic in case he came by to work on the kitchen. Now knowing the right path, she headed for the side door and knocked.

"Sam!" Maddie's voice filled with pleasure as she opened the door. "Come on in. I was just about to put the kettle on." She filled the electric kettle at the sink, then clicked it on. "I've had you on my mind. I got to thinking and called the vet, Zeke Harrison. I described your kitten and he believes she's part of an abandoned litter. They were found near the highway and Zeke's been trying to come up with homes for them. Someone about three blocks away was fostering two of the kittens and one wandered off. Sounds like you can consider her yours."

Relieved, Sam smiled. "I've really gotten attached to Tabby."

"I figured she'd have a name by now." Maddie nodded knowingly. "She'll be good company."

"I bought her a collar," Samantha confessed.

"Good!" Maddie opened a porcelain canister, then frowned. "I forgot I was running so low on supplies."

"I'd offer to let you borrow what you need, but you've heard about the state of my kitchen." Sam held up her small gift. "I brought you some fresh lavender. Rachel picked it up for me. I don't know about putting it in tea, but it has a calming effect."

"Thanks, but don't you need it for yourself?"

"Rachel brought over practically a bushel. I put quite a bit under my pillow. I'm guessing you can use some calm time yourself."

"You're right about that." Maddie glanced back at the canister. "What I really need is a good hour to wander down the aisles and pick out a whole new assortment."

"Why don't you go now?" Sam rolled closer. "I can stay here with your mother."

Doubt entered Maddie's eyes as they traveled over the wheelchair.

"I can't carry her out myself, but I have my cell phone and I can call 911."

"Which Mom doesn't know to do anymore."

"I did manage to get out of a burning house myself." Sam placed a hand over her heart in a criss-cross motion. "Cross my heart, I won't light any stoves, candles or even play with matches."

Maddie chuckled. "I sound like an awful worry-wart, don't I?"

"No. You just care about your mother."

"I hate to take advantage—"

"I offered," Sam reminded her gently. "If you'll trust me, I'd like to do this for you." It had been too long since she'd been able to help anyone other than herself.

Longing fleeted across Maddie's face, then her features eased into pleasure. "You're a lifesaver! I won't be long."

"Take as long as you like. You've got my cell number and you can call to check in, if it'll make you feel better."

"A whole hour to myself," Maddie murmured. "You're a gift."

"Or longer," Sam reminded. "I don't have anywhere to be."

"Mom's asleep." Maddie bit her lip, still considering. "She probably won't wake up until I'm home."

Sam leaned forward. "Then quit stalling and get going."

"The teakettle shuts off automatically," Maddie told her as she grabbed her purse, then fumbled for her keys.

"Go."

Maddie finally did.

It was quiet in the house, the television was off, no music played. Samantha glanced out the front window, which had a similar view as her own. She wondered how many hours Maddie sat here as her life passed by. Yet she wasn't even a touch resentful. When Samantha had tentatively questioned her on their last visit, Maddie had said the Lord was her solace. Swallowing, Sam finally acknowledged the hole in her heart, the missing place where the Lord had resided within.

The phone rang suddenly. Thinking it might be Maddie, Sam answered.

"Sam?" Bret questioned with surprise.

"Yes."

"Is Maddie home?"

"No. She's shopping."

"Oh."

"Do you want me to give her a message?"

Bret hesitated. "Ah, no. It's about a prayer circle. I'll talk to her later."

"Okay." Sam gently replaced the receiver. Seemed prayer was on lots of minds today.

Bret stepped back to check the replastering job he'd just finished in Samantha's kitchen. He wasn't a professional, but the technique looked all right. Mentally, he ticked off the list of the work. Cabinets were coming along. They still had to buy appliances, but his mother had come up with an idea on how to raise money for them. And he should get on with matching the limestone. But he thought Sam ought to have some input into the project, maybe go to the quarry with him.

"Bret?" Rachel called from the living room.

"Be right there."

Rachel didn't wait, instead skirting through the mess in the kitchen. "You need to finish up or you'll be in here when Sam gets home."

Bret had found Sam's note. After learning Maddie was out, he'd called her cell. She was excited to join his plan. Feeling he had enough time, Bret then called Rachel and her parents. The Carrutherses accepted their invitation in an instant.

On a crazy impulse the day before, he'd ordered a cake to celebrate Samantha's first steps. Just a small token. But when he found her note, he realized the milestone required a celebration. And Sam's family could make it a real occasion. Thrilled by the news, they'd all but raced to the house, bringing balloons, noisemakers and sparkling white-grape juice. And his impulse became a full-fledged party.

Bret wiped his hands on a well-used rag, then closed up the plaster bucket. Telling himself that anyone would be impatient, he could hardly wait to see Sam's reaction.

After washing up, Bret joined the others in the living room. Trudy and Rachel were tying balloons in place. And Ethel Carruthers put the final touches on the dining room table. She'd made a quick batch of her cheese puffs, one of Sam's favorites.

"She's coming!" Rachel hollered. Since half the guests weren't all that agile, they'd decided not to try and hide, just to yell "surprise."

Practically holding their breaths, everyone was silent. They could hear the creaking of the ramp, the small thud of wheels as Samantha rolled upward. Even the turning of the doorknob sounded loud.

Samantha pushed open the door, her head down as she navigated over the threshold.

"Surprise!" A half-dozen voices shouted.

Jerking her head up, Sam stared at them in shock. Her mouth opened, but no sound emerged.

Rachel reached Sam first, hugging her cousin. "Congratulations!"

The others crowded around. Samantha accepted more hugs from Trudy, Don and her elderly neighbors. Bret held back, watching. It wouldn't take Samantha long to figure out who had spread the news.

Once she could see past the mini-crowd, Samantha glanced around at the balloons and festive table. "I can't believe all this."

"Believe it." Rachel handed Sam one of the noise-makers, then blew her own, unfurling a feather-capped party favor. "Come see your cake."

Samantha obliged, following Rachel into the dining room. Bret trailed them, wanting to see Sam's reaction.

"Ooh! I can smell Mrs. Carruthers's cheese puffs." Then she reached the table and stared at the cake.

Shaped like a foot, the one-of-a-kind creation even

had manicured toes and a pretty anklet bracelet with her name spelled out in icing.

"My first steps," Sam murmured. Her lips wobbled briefly. "Oh, Rachel, how perfect!"

"Can't take the credit, cuz. Bret thought up the cake—" she waved her arms around "—and all of this."

Sam's gaze met his, her eyes suddenly vulnerable, filling with questions.

"Couldn't let a big step like this go by without celebrating." He added the pun to reduce the tension he saw in her face.

"Step." She nodded, a fraction of the vulnerability fading. "I get it." Samantha paused. "It's really…nice. *Extremely* nice."

Bret was aware of everyone watching. "Thought I'd butter you up before we start on those holiday decorations for Main Street."

"We're so proud of you," Trudy gushed. A mountain of emotion in a small package, Trudy was laughing and crying at the same time.

Don laid his arm over his wife's shoulders. "Sure are. I bet your folks dropped the phone when you told them."

"I haven't yet." Sam hurried to explain. "If I keep doing better, I'd like to surprise them on Thanksgiving."

Trudy's tears flowed openly while Don's misted. "Mighty fine, Samantha."

"Now you've got me going," Rachel chided, wiping her cheeks. "Probably have mascara on my chin."

"I didn't mean to bring the mood down." Sam

looked at them all, her gaze lingering on Bret. "This is such a wonderful surprise."

Rachel tooted her noise maker. "All right, then."

The doorbell rang only moments later. Maddie stood on the front porch, her mother, Lillian, in a wheelchair.

"Come in!" Bret held the door open so Maddie could push the chair inside. "Glad you could make it."

"Mom and I wouldn't have missed it."

The fragile, older woman's eyes lit up at the sight of the balloons. "It's a party?"

"Yes, Mrs. Carter. We're glad you could join us." Bret pecked her wrinkled cheek lightly.

Obviously pleased, Mrs. Carter smiled. "I love parties."

Sam looked confused, but happy to see them. "How'd you all arrange this?"

"You were a big help," Bret replied. "Getting yourself out of the way."

"And giving me a really special treat. I feel like a new, incredibly pampered woman," Maddie added. "Thank you."

Rachel picked up a dessert knife and manned the dining room table. "Who wants cake?" She cut into the moist layers and started passing out slices.

Bret carried two plates, one for Mrs. Carter, one for Maddie.

"Get some for yourself, young man," Mrs. Carter admonished. Then she picked up her fork with a slightly shaky hand. "I love cake."

"Yes, ma'am," he replied with a grin.

Rachel continued handing out generous slices. When she got to the last one, she licked a bit of cake from her fingers. "Yum. Caramel?"

"Sam's favorite," Bret replied.

Seven sets of eyes swung his way. Remembering her likes and dislikes. It had to seem odd to the others. After all, it had been eight years.

He stuck both hands in his pockets. "Couldn't ask her. Would have given away the surprise. She might not even like caramel anymore."

"It's still my favorite," Sam replied quietly.

They used to order one piece of caramel and one of his favorite, chocolate, from the small, local bakery whose speciality was the caramel cake with equally rich caramel frosting. Then he and Sam would share, the best of both worlds. Without her voicing the words, he knew she was recalling the same memory.

"Great choice," Don said heartily, filling the uneasy gap of silence. "I know I'm going to want seconds."

"There's plenty, Dad." Rachel took a piece for herself, then casually strolled over to the DVD player and turned on some soft music.

Unaware of the tension, Mrs. Carter continued to eat her cake, the only person in the room doing so.

Everyone gradually began talking again, the tone of the party brightening. As it improved, Bret watched Sam, who had rolled back up to the table. While the others were distracted, she reached out to trace the outline of the cake. Just then, Tabby jumped up into her lap. Sam buried her face against the tiny kitten's soft fur. But before she did, Bret saw hope. And even a sliver of belief.

When all the Conways were at the nursery, it came alive in a way it never did otherwise. Nancy and Janie had come by to choose materials for their seasonal wreaths. While they lingered over dried grapevines and olive branches, Robert tried to ride herd on the kids.

Bret guessed his mother had drafted his father to watch the children so he wouldn't be left home alone. Robert looked pale, fatigued. Of course, his energetic grandchildren could cause that within a few minutes.

"Hey, Dad. Couldn't think of an excuse fast enough to get out of rugrat detail?"

Robert plopped down on one of the well-worn wooden stools near the counter. "I know I'm old, but I don't remember you and Janie flying around so fast."

Bret grinned. "That's not age, Dad. Only three of them, but it seems like those kids run in half a dozen directions at once." Glancing across the counter, he noticed that Herb was trying to help two customers by himself, while Peter fiddled with seed packets. "Be right back."

Bret assisted the older woman, helping her find the peat moss she was looking for. He was more than ready to trounce Peter, but not while the family was present. His father didn't need to be upset. Still, Bret couldn't let the matter completely slide. "Peter, you can't ignore customers."

"I thought Herbie had everything in hand." Peter didn't look up from the seed packets.

Bret glanced over at his family. "We'll talk later."

"Whatever."

Herb rang up the purchase from the man he'd assisted, then another from a customer who had dashed in for some plant food.

Nancy strolled back to stand beside her husband. "If there's a minute between customers, I want to talk to you more about the fundraiser for Samantha—well, actually, for her whole family. Imagine how her parents would feel if they come home for Thanksgiving and there's only part of a kitchen."

It wouldn't be a tragedy, but Bret knew his mother wasn't letting go of this particular bone.

"I've talked to a few friends," Nancy continued. "We could have a yard sale, maybe a baked-goods sale." Concentrating, she pursed her lips. "Seth's getting a significant discount on the appliances and materials, but it'll still all add up. Anyone have other thoughts on the fundraiser?"

Peter strolled by, his voice casual. "Could sell some plants. That ought to raise a bit."

Since only Herb and Robert knew about the problems with Peter, Nancy and Janie looked at him in confused surprise.

"Mom, why don't we talk about this over dinner one night?" Bret suggested, shooting Peter a warning glare. "I can brainstorm better when I'm not at work."

"Whatever you think, dear."

"I think Dad would probably like a break from kid duty."

Nancy looked over at Robert, trying to hide the concern in her eyes. But Bret was accustomed to ferreting it out over the years. They'd spent far too many hours in hospitals waiting on news about his dad for her to fool him. "You're right, of course."

"You don't have to head up this fundraiser," Bret said quietly, so that only his mother could hear. "You've got enough to worry about."

She patted his arm. "So do you, son. But that's not going to stop us, is it?"

Chapter Twelve

The limestone quarry, situated more than an hour past Rosewood, was dusty. Good and dusty. A front loader scooped up a boulder, raising even more dust. Beyond the machinery, slabs of limestone leaned against a stone wall.

Samantha gripped a piece of limestone cut from the kitchen counter. With Thanksgiving approaching at breakneck speed, she desperately wanted the kitchen to be functional. "Do you really think they'll be able to match this?"

Bret drove past the machinery to a simple stone building. "I talked to the owner—the quarry's been in the same family for generations. From the description I gave him, he thinks they're still mining out of the same pit. There'll probably be some variations, but you know that'd happen with any natural material."

Samantha was nervous. Although the surprise party

had been held over a week ago, she hadn't been able to shake the feelings it had caused.

"Have you considered that maybe change would be good?" Bret asked.

Startled, she jerked toward him. It took her a few moments to realize he was talking about the kitchen. "I know Mom said that she wished some things were more modern, but she was always worried, too, that something new might spoil the look of the house."

"Matt's keeping the cabinet design true to the period. But even he agrees with Seth's changes to the butler's pantry." It was a fancy name for a corridor-like space next to the kitchen that held dishes, glassware and other kitchen necessities. "Seth has designed some stellar houses. I don't think you'll be disappointed."

"Can we just look at the limestone now?"

"The mason's good. He won't try to talk you into something you're not sure about. And Seth will get with him on the measurements."

"We're just going to look, right? You know I don't have the money to order any stone."

"My mother's had an idea about that. She and Janie are organizing a fundraiser. Tag sale or bake sale, something like that."

Grateful, yet embarrassed to be a charity project, Samantha wasn't sure what to say. "I appreciate…" She cleared her throat. "But there are a lot more worthwhile causes than my kitchen. I can't ask your family to go to so much trouble and—"

"You didn't ask. They offered. And you'd have an easier time deterring a Sherman tank than my mother."

Samantha had always liked Bret's mother. She was the kind of person who went out of her way for others…who had treated Sam like a true daughter. Now that she was wise enough to realize it, Sam knew Nancy would be the perfect mother-in-law. "But—"

"We're here to look at the limestone, remember?" He got out of the Blazer, then skirted the hood to open her door. "Just concentrate on the kitchen, okay?"

Samantha kept her grip on their sample as Bret lifted her out of his SUV. Despite her first faltering steps at physical therapy, she wasn't anywhere close to actually walking on her own.

For a moment Bret cradled her next to his chest. She could feel the thud of his heartbeat beneath his soft, thick shirt. And his face was disturbingly near to hers. She remembered the kiss they'd exchanged, gentle but searing. Sam wished she could reach out, run her fingers across his strong jaw. His grip tightened, almost as though he'd read her thoughts. Then he eased her down into the wheelchair. Disappointment flooded through her.

Sam tried to forget the feelings as Bret pushed her chair over the gravel pathway. Making herself concentrate on the limestone, Sam didn't see any that looked even remotely similar to their sample.

A short, thickset man squatted beside one of the slabs.

"That's Dilbert Dunn, the mason who says he can replicate your counters, or any other configuration you want. And he said he can have it ready by Thanksgiving."

Samantha looked at the limestone in dismay. The counters in her parents' house had been rich with embedded colors. These all looked dull and gray.

Bret made the introductions and Sam tried not to let her disappointment show.

"Did you bring a sample?" the mason asked.

Reluctantly, she held out the stone.

"You're lucky. We still mine that pit. Have some I can show you."

He led them to one of the dull-looking slabs.

Sam tried to swallow her disappointment.

Mr. Dunn looked up at her with a knowing sort of amusement. "Not impressed?" He walked over to an outside water spigot and filled a bucket. Back at the limestone, he dipped a cloth into the water, then washed a center spot in the slab. As he rubbed the stone, it gradually came to life, exposing the true color. Warm shades of brown, gold and rust, along with the shimmer of quartz, emerged.

The beauty of the limestone was stunning.

"Not exactly like the piece you're holding there," Mr. Dunn continued. "But it's close. Lot of limestone's come out of that pit since yours. Nature's not a machine. Develops at its own rate."

"So it does," she murmured, entranced by the amazing colors.

"Think this'll do?" Mr. Dunn questioned.

"Oh, yes." Sam could easily envision the beautiful stone paired with native pine. It would be breathtaking.

Bret leaned close. "Impressive work He does."

She looked up. "Mr. Dunn?"

Bret met her eyes, holding the gaze. "The Lord."

Samantha felt the smallness of her own vision.

"That He does," Mr. Dunn chimed in. "Can't take three steps in this part of Texas and not see it." He wiped his hands on the damp cloth. "I'll go inside, write up the order." He left, his boots crunching on the gravel.

In the quiet, Samantha felt the tearing at her heart and spirit.

Unexpectedly, Bret covered one of her hands with his own. "It'll sort itself out, Sam. Like getting out of this chair. It's going to be one step at a time."

"I don't know." She bent her head down to avoid his gaze. So much was overwhelming her. The upcoming visit, her tentative steps, both physical and spiritual, the kiss she had shared with Bret. And…wondering if he would ever see her as a real woman again.

Holiday decorations in Rosewood hadn't changed all that much over the last century, other than the exception of adding lights, with the advent of electricity to the rural area.

But Bret wanted to introduce some of his living Christmas trees into the design, his contribution to the community. With Thanksgiving just around the corner, Sam was stressing about her parents' upcoming visit. Bret thought working on the design would be an effective distraction, especially since all the decorations had to be in place for the Thanksgiving parade.

Standing beside Sam's wheelchair, he pointed to the Victorian street lamps that lined Main Street. "What would you think of putting one of my trees between every two lights?"

"Do you have that many?" Leaning forward to see better, Sam winced.

"You okay?"

"Just moved too fast." She dismissed his concern, tilting her head to study the proportions of the street. "If you have enough trees close in size it would work."

"More trees than customers for them."

Sam looked at him in concern. "Business is off?"

That was a worry she didn't need to share. "I plant new trees every year. It's just convincing people they're worth the trouble of keeping them alive from year to year. I know a lot of environmentalists claim that artificial trees are the best solution. But that means more plastic in the landfills. I can't get behind that."

"And every new tree helps the planet," she murmured in agreement. "You're not just trying to get me off track, are you? I don't want your business to suffer because of me."

He was adjusting again to the fact that being around Samantha was somewhat akin to riding next to a thunderstorm, never knowing when it would stir up. "Let me worry about my business." Bret pulled out a sketch of the street with the usual garlands, wreaths and bows. In the precise middle of Main Street, a large star traditionally hung at the highest point. "I'm not sure just how we'd decorate my trees. Don't want them to clash with what we already have, but I don't want them looking too commercial, too overdone."

"What about getting the kids involved? Have them string popcorn and cranberries. The garlands would look natural and the birds can eat them when it gets colder." She frowned. "Unless kids don't like doing stuff like that anymore."

"Kids are still kids. I can talk to the principal at the church school, see if she thinks it's a viable project."

"And pine cones," Sam mused. "Without any sort of glitter or other junk glued on. You know, just nestled in the branches. But we need something to tie into the other decorations." She reached for the wheels, flinching as she twisted around.

"How'd your therapy go yesterday?"

"Okay. J.C. thinks I can keep building muscle that'll help me move more easily."

"No problem with the exercises?"

She shook her head. "I didn't walk across the gym, if that's what you mean."

It wasn't. He hadn't seen signs of pain before. Exasperation, exhaustion, disinterest. But not pain. "Tomorrow's a regular session?"

"What about stars?" Enthusiasm filled her voice. "On the tops of the trees? Not to take away from the main one, but to reinforce its presence?"

"I'm glad you're getting into the design—"

Sam reached for the sketch. Before she could take it, a spasm of pain shot across her face and she fell back.

"Sam?"

"I must have pinched a nerve. I know—ridiculous. Here I couldn't move my legs, now I manage to pinch a nerve I probably wouldn't have felt before."

Bret wasn't so sure. He'd heard dismissals like hers from his father. And the outcome wasn't always good.

Several days later, Bret still hadn't shed his concern. It was his turn to take Sam to therapy. She was quiet while they traveled to the hospital, then entered the pool area. Harold had suggested a short warm-up to prepare for the parallel bars.

Needing to feel her close, Bret lifted Sam from her chair and carried her down the ramp instead of using the PVC wheelchair that could roll down into the water. He savored the soft nestle of Samantha's arms around his neck, the feel of her long, dark hair against his cheek.

Easing Sam into the water, he immediately missed the contact. She usually paddled forward as soon as she was in the pool, arms working at high speed. Today, however, she barely broke the surface of the water with a half-hearted breaststroke.

"Not in the mood to do your exercises?"

"Just a little tired," she admitted, moving her legs slowly.

"Do you want to reschedule your session with Harold?"

She shook her head. "Won't get anywhere if I start

doing that." Still, she wasn't attempting any of the normal water exercises, instead staying on the shelf, moving only her arms.

Thirty minutes went by slowly. Quietly. As Bret debated talking to Harold about canceling today's session, Wanda came over. "I'm free now if you're ready to get out, Samantha."

"Thank you." Sam looked relieved.

While Wanda waited, Bret lifted Samantha. As he carried her up the ramp, she sagged against him. She hadn't done that since the first days of her aqua therapy.

While Wanda helped Samantha, Bret quickly changed into dry clothes. He was going to have that word with Harold.

But the therapist wasn't anywhere in sight. As Bret considered looking for him in the hospital cafeteria, Wanda pushed Samantha's chair into the large exercise room. Harold was directly behind them. No way to have a private conversation.

Still, Sam looked a little more invigorated. Maybe he was making too much of what he'd seen. But his gut didn't unclench.

Harold assisted Samantha in getting up from her wheelchair. Her face paled slightly, but she smiled. A forced smile.

Once upright, Sam grabbed hold of the parallel bars. Rachel had reported that in the last session, Samantha had managed to take two additional steps. Although they hadn't had another party to celebrate, the mood of Sam's family and friends was high, hopeful.

Bret watched intently.

Sam licked her lips, then swallowed. She followed with a deep breath. Then she stared down at her feet. Determination filled her features.

His gaze sharpened. She wasn't yet trying to move her feet.

Sam raised her head. Lips compressed into a tight line, she picked up her right foot. Pain streaked across her face, but she didn't stop. Sheer force of will took over, and Sam lifted her left foot. As she did, the pain clearly intensified. Unable to control her expression or her body, she crumpled, her head striking the tile floor.

Bret sprang to her side. Harold reached her only seconds later.

Her breathing shallow, Sam's eyes remained closed.

Bret looked to Harold for reassurance. But the therapist was calling for help. Bret followed as they wheeled her to the emergency room, where J.C. met them.

Bret had a thousand questions, but J.C. waved him back. "I'll talk to you when I know something."

The waiting room outside Emergency wasn't full. Mostly family members, a few who looked anxious, some who flipped through magazines. Bret tried to sit, but found he couldn't. Time crawled by. He worried about how long they were taking. If it wasn't anything serious, J.C. should have come out by now and given him a report.

Glancing again at his watch, Bret resisted the urge to check with the nurse. From his days of waiting in hospitals while his father had numerous surgeries,

Bret knew the doctor would come out when there was something to report. Not before.

He stood to one side of the automatic double doors that led to the inner sanctum. Knowing an ambulance could arrive at any time, Bret didn't block the doors, but he wanted to be as close as possible.

The doors whooshed open and J.C. stepped out. His expression was sober, but not ominous. "She's stable. Passed out from the pain. Initial X-rays revealed an anomaly near the point of injury. Looks like she has a concussion as well—don't know how serious. I've ordered a series of tests. Once we get all the results, I'll have a clearer picture."

"She was hurting yesterday. Said she thought it was a pinched nerve."

J.C. nodded. "Pain increases with movement, stress to the impact. Between the pressure on her sciatic nerve from the herniated disks and some kind of foreign object lodged near the injury site…"

"Can I see her?"

"Sam's already on her way to get an MRI. Depending on the outcome, I want to give her some pain medication. She'll probably be out for awhile. Why don't you go home, come back in the morning?" J.C. patted his shoulder in reassurance, then headed down the hall.

J.C. was right. Leaving would be the sensible thing to do. He had plenty of work piled up. Instead, Bret glanced again at his watch. Wouldn't take forever to get an MRI. And despite the effects of the pain medication, once he saw her, Bret would be able to tell how Sam was doing. He always had.

Why was there fog in the house? Was it another fire? Was it smoke, not fog? Sam squinted, trying to shut out the piercing sunlight. How could the sun shine when it was foggy?

She tried to turn her face so she could look to one side. Her head weighed a thousand pounds. Oh, now she remembered. The ice. She'd fallen and couldn't move. Not even her head.

But she *could* move her head. Ever since that day. Only her legs didn't work. Or did they? Concentrating, she tried to wiggle her toes. For a terrifying moment, she felt nothing. Then a flicker of movement.

She was so very tired. It took ages, but millimeter by millimeter, she forced her head to turn. A man was sprawled in the chair beside her bed. Squinting again, she tried to make out his face. Bret? But that couldn't be. He was still in Rosewood.

Confused, she sighed.

And he bolted up from the chair as though set on fire.

"Samantha? Can you hear me?"

Of course. She wasn't deaf. But the words didn't come out aloud. She tried to lick her lips, but her mouth was too dry. "What…?" The solitary word wobbled.

"Do you remember your therapy session today?" He stared into her eyes, his own dark with worry.

Again she tried to wet her lips and failed.

He turned away for a moment, returning with something cold that he placed gently on her mouth. "Ice chips. J.C. said you can drink some water when you're awake enough. He gave you some pretty strong medicine after your tests."

She sucked on the ice chip, letting it melt in her mouth, trying to make sense of what Bret was saying.

He gave her a second piece of ice, this time easing it over her lips before letting it go. "J.C. said he'll talk to you in the morning. Your family came by."

"Mom and Dad?"

"Rachel left a little while ago. She and her parents will be here in the morning."

How could it be night? The sun was still shining. She squinted against the brightness.

"I asked the nurse to dim the lights, but she keeps flipping them back on." He stepped away for a moment and the brightness disappeared. "Just the side lamp is better."

"Bret?" Her voice still sounded strange.

"You want some more ice?" He picked up a cup from the table next to the bed. "J.C. said the medicine would make your mouth dry." He gave her another piece of ice. "Surprised you woke up. They told me you'd sleep through the night."

"Where…?"

"Same hospital you had your session in."

"Session?"

He frowned, his eyebrows pulling together.

Was he mad? Of course he was. He'd never stopped being angry.

The nurse stepped in, switching the lights back on. Sam tried to close her eyes against them.

"So we've woken up?" The cheery nurse asked in a singsong voice. "Let's get your temp and blood pressure." She went through the ritual, noting the results in the computer next to the bed. Smiling, she turned back to Samantha. "Any pain?"

"No..."

The woman nodded. "Dr. Mueller left orders for continued pain medication." She checked the intravenous drip. "I'll turn it down a bit." She picked up the call buzzer. "Just push this if the pain returns."

Dr. Mueller? Some of the fuzziness in her brain dissipated. J.C. Andy's friend. In Rosewood. She was home in Rosewood. "Why...am I here?"

"Had a little incident while you were in therapy."

Therapy. Bit by bit, reality returned. She'd tried to walk and the pain had been excruciating. After that, everything remained cloudy. Turning her head slightly, she fixed her gaze on Bret. Who had stayed since she'd fallen. What? Hours ago?

Concern remained in his eyes, in the stiff language of his body.

But why? He'd been done with caring about her years ago. Hadn't he?

Chapter Thirteen

The following morning J.C. sat next to Samantha's bed, flipping through her chart. Bret, Don, Trudy and Rachel stood at attention, waiting for the verdict.

"A bone fragment was overlooked in your initial surgery for the fractured vertebrae," J.C. announced.

"That doesn't sound too bad...." Rachel's words trailed away.

Samantha looked up at J.C. for confirmation. But his expression didn't lighten. "What does that mean?" Had she been a fool to believe that she could walk again?

"Another surgery to remove it."

Sam was glad most of the pain medication had worn away so she could think more clearly. "What if I don't have the surgery?"

J.C. closed the chart. "The pain will only increase."

"If I push past it?"

He looked down for a moment. "The pain won't go away. It's manageable while you're immobile. But not if you want to continue therapy. You'd need so much medication, it would put you to sleep. Therapy isn't an option without the surgery."

Sam closed her eyes to escape the expectant faces circling her. She hadn't admitted it to herself, but she'd begun to hope, to believe she might be able to walk again. Having taken those few steps…. It was so unfair. Two steps forward, a hundred back.

Idiotically, she'd let hope seep back into her life. After losing Andy, she'd promised herself never to believe in miracles. It was as though the Lord was letting her know, without a shred of doubt, there would be no heavenly help.

Trudy pushed past her husband to clasp Samantha's hand. "Sam, I want you to listen to me. I'm going to say what your mother would if she were here. Let's put this situation in perspective. The doctor did *not* say you would never walk again. He said you need surgery. You have to have faith that everything will work out."

"Faith?" Sam couldn't expunge the bitterness and self-pity that accompanied the word.

"Yes." Bret took a step forward, inching in front of J.C. "It comes one step at a time, remember?"

It wasn't fair! She'd worked so hard, had so many treatments, so many tests. She'd tackled the pain, tried to get past it. Glancing up, she met Bret's steady gaze. His eyes were filled with challenge and…was that belief?

"He's right," Rachel encouraged.

Biting back tears, Sam gathered her voice. "And this operation…how bad will it be?"

"Don't think in terms of *bad*," J.C. cautioned with a touch of kind reproof. "I won't say it's routine. There are risks in any surgery, but I wouldn't recommend the operation if I didn't think it was the right choice."

Risks. As though that would stop her. "How soon would I recover?"

J.C. chuckled. "Glad to see you're back. In answer to your question—awhile."

Thanksgiving was a week away. When her parents would be home. "What's awhile?"

"Depends. Anywhere from three to six weeks."

Samantha shook her head. "No."

Scrunching his forehead in confusion, J.C. frowned. "Why? If it's the money—"

"Of course, but that's not all." Don and Trudy had helped pay for medical care that hadn't been donated or supplied by volunteers. But surgery was a whole different level of cost. "My parents are coming home for Thanksgiving. I want them to see that I'm better, to show them how much progress I've made. That won't happen if I'm lying in the hospital."

"But—" A flurry of voices chorused.

Couldn't they understand? "No buts. And no operation until they're back in Africa."

"Honey, are you sure?" Trudy smoothed the hair back on Sam's forehead. "They'll see that you're in pain."

Samantha turned her gaze on J.C.

"The pain can be managed on a short-term basis. But

any sort of movement will trigger it. Again, medicine strong enough to block the pain will take you out."

"What if I don't go to therapy?" Sam desperately wanted her parents to enjoy this visit, worry free.

Reluctantly, J.C. nodded. "They'll be here, what? A week? No therapy this week or next, then we schedule the operation."

Swallowing, Sam shut out all the possible complications, ones J.C. hadn't verbalized. What if the operation terminated the small movement she'd attained? "No therapy," she replied, avoiding his reference to the surgery.

"We'll talk more." Clearly J.C. hadn't missed her evasiveness.

"Maybe we should let you get some rest." Trudy fussed with Samantha's pillows, then straightened the blanket. "Can we bring you anything?"

Samantha shook her head.

"Can she have ice cream?" Rachel asked.

J.C. looked up from the chart he still held. "Sure. I'll be back to check on you later, Sam."

"I'll bring you some chocolate-chocolate-chip," Rachel promised.

As the small herd dispersed, Bret remained behind. Now out of the deep trenches of pain medication, Samantha pondered on his unusual actions. She wouldn't have been surprised to wake up in the hospital to find Rachel sitting with her. But Bret....

Had he come to pity her? She'd prefer anger over pity. He adjusted the blinds so that some light could enter the room, but not shine in her eyes. Pausing, Bret then turned.

And Samantha couldn't read his expression.

Still, as he neared, she felt a flutter that had nothing to do with pain or the medication she was taking for it. "You didn't have to stay," she blurted out.

"No."

"But then you've never done anything you didn't want to," Sam babbled. "I mean in general."

His eyebrows lifted.

"I wasn't counting on a setback," she confessed, trying to cover her remark. "Especially such a big one."

"You could think of it as a blip."

She frowned. "That's pretty callous."

"Didn't mean it that way. But dwelling on the negative won't help. You've been doing better. Way better than you thought. Yeah, this surgery...." He shrugged his shoulders. "It's another thing to get through. But you will. A few months ago you thought you'd never walk, never get out of that chair. In the whole scheme of things, it's not as bad as it could be."

Already sobered, Sam reflected on his words, then looked down, fiddling with the blanket. "I must look like a fool. Feeling sorry for myself and—"

"You wouldn't be human if you didn't feel this isn't fair. But a fool? No. Never a fool."

So slowly it barely seemed there was movement, she raised her face. "But—"

"You don't need me to flood you with sympathy. Your family, your friends...of course we think it's a rotten break. But not something you can't handle. Sam, you're ferocious, fearless. If I thought for a second that you wouldn't come out of this all right, I'd tell you."

She still clutched the bit of blanket in her hands. "Then why did you stay last night?"

His mesmerizing brown eyes darkened further, then it looked as though he drew a shade on his feelings. "Nobody should wake up in a hospital, not knowing what happened, where they are."

Sam glanced down again, to hide the sharp burst of disappointment. For one stupid moment she'd actually thought it might mean that he still cared. That there was hope, that stupid ridiculous emotion she'd sworn off.

"Samantha?"

She shook her head. "Guess the medication hasn't worn off yet."

"J.C. said you're still on a mild dose." Bret shifted. "I need to get over to your house and meet the stonemason. Your counters are going in today. Matt supervised yesterday. The cabinets are incredible. They turned out even better than we expected. At this rate, looks like the place will be finished by Thanksgiving."

She'd completely blanked out the kitchen, the fact that it needed to be done by the time her parents arrived. She lifted one hand to her face, forgetting about the plastic oxygen meter attached to her finger, clunking it against her nose.

"Whoa. You're still hooked up to a bunch of stuff."

He leaned closer, examining her face. "You left a red mark on the bridge of your nose."

Feeling like an ugly bug under a super-sized microscope, she tried to turn away.

But Bret touched her face, his fingers igniting of trail of fire as he traced a path to her nose. "Doesn't look like it'll bruise." He paused, his face disturbingly close to hers.

Sam held her breath.

The moment stretched out so long she wondered if she'd ever be able to breathe again.

"But the bump on the back of your head's a doozy."

Unable to find her voice, Sam could only look at him.

He eased back. Immediately bereft, she missed his touch.

"Sam…"

She waited.

A different nurse breezed into the room. "Test time."

"Test?" Sam echoed.

"Dr. Mueller wants to keep a close eye on that head injury." The nurse laughed at her own mixed metaphor. "Heard you took quite a fall."

As the nurse crowded closer, Bret shifted back. Sam strained to see him.

He lifted one hand. "Be back later."

"Later," she murmured.

Once he was out of the room, the nurse wriggled her eyebrows in a conspiratorial, knowing way. "Your husband's one handsome guy."

"He's…" She swallowed. "He's not my husband."

"Well, I'd grab him quick. He won't last very long on the open market."

No. One day some woman, some wiser, kinder woman would agree to marry him. And the woman would realize that Bret Conway was more important than anything else. And Sam would be left with the shards of her regret and little else.

Thanksgiving at the Conways' was always a noisy affair. Bret's mother invited friends, extended family and any strays who didn't have holiday plans. She cooked for days, insisting on including everyone's favorites. That meant at least five kinds of potatoes, but she wouldn't have it any other way.

Janie, Herb and their children had arrived early so that Janie could help her mother. She'd promptly left Herb in charge of the kids, and assigned Bret as his assistant.

The smell of roasting turkey blended with that of fresh rolls and tart cranberries.

"I keep telling Janie that sandwiches would be easier." Herb lifted his youngest from the clutches of Nancy's antique curio cabinet. Their three-year-old, Jason, and Nancy's delicate china were not a good match.

Robert joined them in the living room. "Just escaped with my life. Every holiday gets crazier. At this rate, we're going to have to install another stove."

"How many extras did Mom invite this year?"

His father rolled his eyes. "I'm afraid to count. Janie's in charge of the table so I guess she has the official number."

Herb released Jason, who raced off to join his brother and sister.

"I tried to snitch a bite of ham and nearly lost a hand," Robert continued. "And there are enough pies in there to start a bakery."

"Janie and Nancy are enlarging the fundraiser idea for Sam," Herb told them. "They've recruited half the town. Now it's up to a bazaar. Tag sale, food, crafts. Half the women in church are making hand goods. Maddie Carter's crocheting one of her afghans that always sells for a lot. They're determined to raise enough for Sam's surgery."

Robert balanced the mug of coffee on his knee. "That's what people did when I got my transplant. Couldn't have had the surgery otherwise."

Bret studied his dad's face. It seemed more than tired, more than just pale. His eyes were clouded in a way Bret recognized from the times when Robert was ill. "You getting enough sleep lately?"

Robert chuckled. "Son, you've got enough on your hands without trying to diagnose me. I'm fine. You have Peter to worry about…well, the whole business. Then, of course, there's Sam."

Yes, there was Sam. Bret wondered how it was going at the Shaws'. Her parents should have arrived the day before. And he hadn't wanted to intrude. The Shaws' gathering would be a smaller celebration. Don, Trudy, Rachel, Ed, Joyce and Samantha. Both sets of grandparents were deceased and there wasn't any extended family.

He knew that Trudy had offered to cook. With the dedicated help of all the volunteers, the kitchen was complete. And since they'd decided to hold one big fundraiser instead of separate ones for the kitchen and medical expenses, Don had kicked in the extra money for the discounted appliances. When the stonemason, Mr. Dunn, heard about the circumstances, he gave them the limestone at cost as well.

Bret glanced up as his nephews ran through the adjoining hallway, squealing loudly.

"Better see what they're up to." Herb scrambled out of the room.

Robert sipped his coffee. "You're awfully quiet, son."

"Just thinking about Samantha. It's a big day for her."

"How'd her parents like the renovations?"

Bret shrugged. "Don't know."

"Didn't you call her last night? See how things are going?"

"It was for family." He had started to call more than a dozen times, but never completed dialing her number.

"Once you were practically a member of that family."

"Long time ago." Bret shifted, planting his feet against the hearth.

"So, you've been helping Samantha just because you have so many spare hours? Not enough to do? No business worries?" Robert's eyes were wise, knowing. "And that's why you stayed with her at the hospital?"

They had always been so close that his father could zero in on what was left unsaid. "What was I supposed to do, Dad? Let her fend for herself?"

Robert patted Bret's shoulder. "I'm a lucky man. You've always been responsible, known the right path to take. I don't think that's changed a mite. Seems you've been tapping into your foresight, too. Until today."

Bret frowned.

"There's a time to give people space," Robert continued. "And a time to remember what the Lord would have you do. How do you imagine her folks are feeling? Scared? Afraid to leave her alone for another second? You could set their minds at ease."

"Sam says she won't have the operation unless they go back to Africa," Bret admitted.

"And how do you suppose that makes her parents feel?"

Bret sighed. "Not good."

"A parent never gets over the need to protect. Even when they're lucky enough to have a son who trades roles, takes care of his family."

Uncomfortable with the praise, Bret looked down at the aged, oak floor.

"It's not a weakness to help someone who hurt you in the past. Takes a lot more strength to stay than to walk away."

Swallowing, Bret leaned back. "And when she's better?"

"I can't see into the future any more than you can. But you can pray about it, son. See what the Lord wants for you."

"Sam's stopped believing."

Robert didn't look very surprised. "She's had some

pretty rough breaks. Losing Andy, then facing permanent paralysis. It would break stronger people than Sam. Another reason she needs you. You can help her find her way back."

"Dad…" Bret hesitated. "You didn't advise me to wait for Sam when she left."

"I didn't know the future then, either." Robert took another swallow of coffee. "I do know that when some people love, it's forever."

Bret felt the truth of his father's words, a truth he didn't want to acknowledge. But he didn't believe Sam had held on to their love. "And some don't."

Samantha fussed over the napkins she was folding. It was the only task the other women would allow her to perform. Trudy and Rachel had shopped for and prepared most of the food. Mrs. Carruthers had brought over homemade rolls. But Joyce insisted on making her special sweet potatoes—which happened to be Sam's favorite.

Since her parents' arrival the previous afternoon, everything had seemed surreal. They acted as though they weren't a bit tired despite the long, grueling journey. Then all their excitement and declarations that Sam looked so much better. *Fuller*, her mother had said. *Healthier*, her dad added.

Enough pain medication had allowed Sam to smile through the constant chatter and catching up. By bedtime she felt like a zombie. One that was still in a wheelchair. She'd allowed herself to believe that she could be on her feet, even if only for a few steps at a time. So that her parents would believe she was going to be all right.

"Oh, Sam, the kitchen…it's better than I ever dreamed it could be," her mother repeated. Joyce had been ecstatic about the improvements and couldn't stop talking about the changes. "I wouldn't have thought to put in roll-out shelves, or to change some of the cabinets to drawers. And the new pantry! It feels completely decadent. Imagine, a second sink! You put so much thought into every detail, sweetie."

Guiltily, Sam remembered the contributions from Don, Bret, Matt, Seth, the stonemason. "Well, it wasn't just—"

"It's beautiful, isn't it?" Trudy enthused. "Makes me want to remodel. Of course, then I'd look like a copycat."

Joyce waved one hand. "Don't be silly. Who cares about that?"

"I *could* keep my sandstone," Trudy mused. "That would look different."

Sam exchanged a wry glance with Rachel. Her cousin would be drafted if Trudy went through with the idea.

"When are Maddie and her mother supposed to be here?" Rachel questioned.

"I suggested around noon so they can visit before lunch is ready." Sam slipped an old silver napkin ring in place. "They don't get out that much."

Joyce leaned over to kiss Samantha's forehead. "It's a lovely idea. I've always thought it was a shame that Lillian Carter suffered an early stroke. She's such a sweet woman. Maddie must be relieved that it's not Alzheimer's."

"No sense in Maddie cooking just for the two of them," Samantha demurred. Relocating Tabby to the other side of her lap, she had to smile. The kitten had intensified her habit of clinging. Now Tabby was practically Velcroed to her clothes. She petted the kitten's soft fur, grateful that Bret had taken care of the little cat while she'd been in the hospital. Sam had nearly forgotten about Tabby. But Bret hadn't.

Not wanting to go there, Sam turned to grab another napkin. Immediately she felt a stab of pain. Her medication was adequate only if she was completely still. J.C. hadn't exaggerated the amount of pain she would experience.

It was a small price to pay for having the entire family together. And, for the day, she didn't intend to even think about the surgery, that if something went wrong she'd never walk again. If this was the last holiday she had with even partial movement, she was going to make the most of it. Because there weren't any do-overs. There was no taking back the accident…or choosing to stay in Rosewood with the man she'd always loved.

Chapter Fourteen

By late afternoon on Thanksgiving day, the Conway house was filled with sated guests, a dozen conversations, stuffed tummies, sleepy children and enough pie to feed half the town. Bret passed on his favorite— pecan. Despite the exceptional cooking, he didn't have his usual appetite for holiday food. Instead, he escaped the merriment, slipping into his Blazer.

The streets were quiet, families all tucked inside their homes. Bret didn't have a specific plan, but found himself driving toward Samantha's. He wouldn't go in, he decided. Just glide by to make sure nothing looked amiss. Didn't want that kitten of hers to wander off.

Slowing down, he saw that Ed, Sam's father, stood on the front porch. The older man waved, apparently spotting him at the same time.

So much for gliding by. Bret parked in front of the house behind Rachel's car. Ed walked down the steps of the porch, meeting him halfway.

"Been too long," Ed began. "I was hoping I'd get to see you."

Bret accepted the older man's still strong handshake. "Sam sure is glad you and Mrs. Shaw could come for Thanksgiving."

Ed chuckled quietly. "If I told you it took two mules, a mail truck, a train and then a two-day airplane ride, would you be surprised?"

Bret grinned. "Nope. But impressed."

"Joyce has been so antsy about this trip I thought she might take off without the plane." Ed scratched his head. "Can't believe how good Samantha looks. Last time I saw her, she was white as snow. She actually has color in her face now."

"Helps that she started eating again. Guess you know she hoped to be out of the wheelchair by today."

"Don filled me in on the surgery she needs." Ed sighed. "Expected Sam to bring it up, but she hasn't yet."

"Maybe she wants to forget about it for today. Make it a good holiday."

"I never figured on Sam coming back home. Sure pulled one over on us."

Bret nodded, knowing the older man didn't need to hear the grim details of her first days.

"Can't tell you how much it means to us that you've been helping our girl. The porch ramp, two doors she can get out of by herself." Ed paused. "After Sam called us the first time, one of the neighbors sent a clipping from the paper. Thought we knew what had happened. Joyce was ready to fly back that day. But Don and

Trudy told us you were watching out for her, fixing up the house so it would be safe, taking her to the doctor, getting her started on therapy." Ed swallowed. "I've always thought you were a good man. Hoped Sam would wake up and see what she was missing."

The fact that she hadn't resonated between the men.

"I'm guessing she's learned a lot the last few months," Ed continued. "About home, friends…the things that count."

Bret couldn't give Ed all the reassurances he needed. If Sam recovered, she'd probably head back to New York, her twitching of wanderlust reignited.

Ed met Bret's gaze. "I feel safer knowing you're watching out for Samantha. She might be too stubborn to admit it, but I'm not."

"That stubbornness has been a blessing." Bret shook his head wryly. "She still can't back down from a challenge. Makes it easy to goad Sam into taking better care of herself."

Grinning, Ed nodded. "That's my girl."

And once, Bret's girl.

"You'll come inside," Ed continued. "We still have lots of pie."

"You, too?"

Ed chuckled. "The women overdo, don't they? We've got enough dessert in there for us each to have our own pie."

"Kitchen okay?" Bret asked, trying to wiggle out of the invitation.

"Could hardly believe it was ours. Joyce's been

hankering to fix up the kitchen for years. But with spending all our time away, didn't seem practical."

Don opened the front door. "You might as well surrender, Bret. They know you're here."

Ed clapped a hand on Bret's shoulder. "Don and I need reinforcements. Women have us outnumbered three to one."

Choices gone, Bret quietly followed the men inside. He didn't immediately see Sam.

But Joyce spotted him. She rushed over, arms outstretched. "You're a sight for sore eyes."

He returned her hug. It wasn't difficult. He'd always liked Sam's parents.

"I'm so glad you stopped by," Joyce continued, her voice bright. "We have tons of dessert!"

Bret tried to look enthusiastic. "I heard."

Joyce sent her husband a knowing glance. "I'll bet. Do you have room for some coffee?"

"Sure."

"The girls are in the kitchen," Joyce told him, referring to the younger generation. "The old folks are catching up out here."

Trudy took a mug from the dining room breakfront, then filled it with coffee. "We won't make you choose."

He accepted the mug, allowing it to warm his hands.

Lillian Carter patted the empty sofa spot next to her.

"How are you doing, Mrs. Carter?"

Lillian smiled as sweetly as she always had. "I'm fine, young man."

Bret didn't remind her of his name, knowing she would forget it in moments.

"Maddie made both apple and pecan pies— Lillian's recipes." Joyce ticked the choices off on her fingers. "And we have pumpkin, cherry, mincemeat and cheesecake."

He smiled at Mrs. Carter. "Guess I'll have to try the pecan."

Trudy reached for another dessert plate and cut him a generous piece. He started to rise and she waved him back, bringing over the slice of pie. "Here you go."

Bret took a bite, then nodded. "Mrs. Carter, pecan pie's my favorite, and this one's wonderful."

"I'll have to get the recipe." Lillian smiled. "I love making pies."

Joyce sat down in a chair close by. "Lillian and I were talking about when Maddie and Samantha were in school. Doesn't seem that long ago."

Bret's fork paused midair. "Probably does to Sam."

Joyce's eyes filled with understanding. "We appreciate everything you've done, Bret. I don't think I could have stayed away this long if I hadn't known you were taking care of her."

"Sam's still strong. She just had to find that out for herself."

Ed walked over to perch on the arm of his wife's chair. "Thanks for reminding her."

"Coffee's done," Rachel announced, clicking off the brewer. "The carafe's probably empty by now. I'll go fill it up." She swished through the new bypass that led directly out of the kitchen into the dining room. It was an improvement they all loved.

Maddie dried a large platter and put it on the counter. "You can stop pretending you feel all right."

Smiling, Sam tried to ignore the excruciating pain in her back. "What do you mean?"

"I do a lot of pretending myself," Maddie reminded her quietly.

Sam slumped back. "I just want to get through today."

"To make it a great Thanksgiving for your parents." Maddie reached for a bowl. "And for us. I really appreciate the invitation. Especially when you have so much on your mind right now."

"Maddie…can I ask you…how you cope? I mean…well, you've been taking care of your mother for years now."

The other woman finished drying the bowl and carefully set it beside the platter. "It's not always easy. But I take it one day at a time…"

As Bret kept telling her to do.

"And…there's a verse I turn to when I can't cope. I don't know it word for word. It comes from Second Corinthians. But the essence is, "We are hard pressed on every side, but not crushed; perplexed, but not driven to despair; persecuted, but not abandoned; struck down, but not destroyed." I think about Paul, what an overwhelming mission he had, that he clearly felt its pressure. Yet he coped."

"But, well…what if it is? More than I can deal with, I mean."

Maddie smiled wisely. "Sam, the Lord's always with us, whether we're listening or not. And He carries us when we can't carry ourselves."

The thought brought instant tears, even though she resisted them.

Maddie knelt down so she was at eye level. "I don't have all the answers. Not by any means. But I do know the Lord loves you—that never changes. And, He'll be with you when you have the surgery."

"It may not work," Sam whispered.

"And it might," Maddie insisted. "No matter how it turns out, your family and friends will love you just as much as they do right this minute."

Embarrassed, Sam wiped the moisture from her cheeks.

"We're all imperfect vessels in perfect hands." Maddie met Sam's eyes. "*All* of us."

"You're a saint, Maddie."

"Nowhere close. Just an imperfect believer."

The following day, Joyce and Ed puttered around the house, enjoying the feel of home. Although the new kitchen still wowed them, they settled in the familiar comfort of the front porch, easing into the old rockers. It was a crisp autumn day. Not cold, just that telltale difference in the air that foretold of one season slipping into the next.

"As much as I love the school kids…" Joyce paused.

"It'll be wonderful to spend Christmas at home with our own Samantha."

Ed leaned back in his rocker. "Two different worlds."

Just inside the open doorway, Sam frowned. She didn't like the turn of their conversation. Ignoring the pain, she rolled out to the porch.

"Good morning, honey." Her dad put his cup down. "I'll get you some coffee."

She waved him back. "No. I mean, in a little bit. Right now we need to talk."

Joyce and Ed exchanged a significant glance.

"What's this about you being here for Christmas?" Sam questioned.

Her parents looked at each other again.

"I'm not twelve. I know something's up."

Ed met her gaze squarely. "We know about the operation. Doesn't matter how. All that matters is we're here for you."

Sam looked at them warily. "You're scheduled to fly out Monday morning."

Joyce shook her head. "No. You need us."

"You had to shut down the school for this trip, right? For a holiday the kids there don't even celebrate. And now you're planning to keep it closed, for what… more than another month, maybe two? No."

"But—"

"I love that you want to do this for me, but the kids in the school need you more. I'll be fine."

Joyce's face filled with distress. "You need someone to take care of you!"

The words were barely out of her mouth when Bret's SUV came into view, then turned into the driveway.

Sam drew her eyebrows together in agitation. "Did you call him?"

Ed sighed. "No. But from what I hear, he's been helping you get settled in, getting you to the doctor and therapy."

Sam leaned back, her mouth opening in exasperation. "So, someone's been talking a *lot*."

"Not to hurt you," Joyce protested.

Bret climbed out of the Blazer and crossed over to the porch. "Morning." He looked at their tense faces and stepped back. "I'm just going to grab my thermos. Leave you all to have some time together without a crowd."

"No." The anger in Sam's solitary declaration was as clear as the beautiful Hill Country day.

Bret looked at Joyce and Ed, ostensibly for a clue.

"So," Sam continued. "You had to tell my parents everything. From your heroic rescue to dragging me to the doctor. Oh, and you didn't leave out how you got me into therapy, fixed up the house, and—"

"Samantha, that's enough." Ed's tone was one Sam remembered from childhood. "Bret didn't tell us anything. Your family is concerned. As they should be. Enough to tell us what's being going on. You expect to have major surgery, then somehow take care of yourself. Surgery you didn't bother to tell us about."

Swallowing, Sam bit back a torrent of words she knew she would regret. "No problem. If you don't go back to Africa, I won't have the surgery."

"Samantha!" Appalled, Joyce stared at her daughter.

Bret sighed, then stepped forward. "We've been talking—Rachel, Don, Trudy. We can all help. Even Maddie's offered her help—said she'll bring Lillian with her. Sorry, Sam. Didn't want to spoil Thanksgiving for you. We knew you wanted it to be the perfect holiday. Looks like we shouldn't have held out on you."

Feeling as helpless and trapped as she had months earlier, Sam turned the fury of her emotions on Bret. "I can't believe you were all talking behind my back, deciding this. Am I mental cripple now, too?"

"Samantha, you've always been a strong woman." Ed's voice gentled. "That's usually an asset. But it makes it hard to ask for help, even when you need it. No one's been plotting. You're blessed to have people who love you this much."

Sam jerked her face back toward Bret. Her fury gone as quickly as it had flared, she felt her lips tremble. If only. But she'd thrown that love away.

Bret didn't immediately break the gaze. Finally, he turned to her parents. "Mr. and Mrs. Shaw, will you be comfortable returning to Africa, knowing Sam's got a whole roster of caregivers?"

Caregiver. The pit in Samantha's stomach plummeted. Had she become so pitiful that Bret saw himself in that position?

"We really want to stay…" Joyce's voice trailed away when Ed took her hand.

"The most important thing is that Samantha has the operation. And she says she won't get it if we don't go back. We trust you, Bret." Ed squeezed Joyce's hand. "And we're grateful for all you've done." He turned to Samantha. "So, will you have the surgery?"

Still numb, Sam lifted her eyes, meeting twin gazes of concern. "I guess so."

Bret exhaled, then spoke to her parents. "Sorry to spoil the morning. But I'm not sure we could keep walking on eggshells the rest of your visit."

The words delivered another blow. Sam felt about as significant as one of the leaves drifting from the trees.

He turned back to meet her eyes. "You okay?"

Sam pulled on her inner strength, which had been tested and battered, but never completely demolished. "Of course. Why wouldn't I be?"

A soft breeze lilted through the air. Several leaves tumbled from the trees, then nestled in a growing pile. To be buried beneath the next ones that fell to the ground. Confirming all of Samantha's doubts.

Chapter Fifteen

Thanksgiving was the traditional kickoff to the holiday season in Rosewood. Which made the timing of the bazaar perfect. Books, baked goods, jams and tag-sale items filled several tables. People buzzed around, admiring the handmade tablecloths, pot-holders, quilts and crafts.

"Oh, Nancy, it's wonderful of you," Joyce exclaimed, looking at the crowded church hall. The event spilled out on to the grounds, the turnout even larger than they'd hoped. "Putting this together."

Nancy waved away the words. "I remember you doing your part when Robert had his transplant."

Impulsively Joyce hugged Nancy. "Our families have been through a lot together. You know I wish it had turned out differently for Bret and Sam. I've always loved that boy."

"Who knows?" Nancy tipped her head to one side.

Joyce gripped her friend's hands. "I've been praying…"

Nancy smiled. "Me, too."

"A lot of people wouldn't be so generous. Sam hurt Bret badly."

"That was a long time ago. And he's had his hands full all these years. Between watching out for his father and me, running the business…well, it's a lot."

Joyce nodded soberly. "Yet he's made time to help Sam. Nancy, about Robert…is his health good?"

Nancy glanced away for a moment. "Good might be an exaggeration. He's had some…episodes, but he gets better. Then there'll be another episode. But that's pretty much how it is for transplant patients."

Joyce squeezed Nancy's hands again.

Maddie Carter pushed her mother's wheelchair up to them. Although Lillian could walk, she was unsteady. "I can't believe how many people turned out!"

"The silent auction on your afghan has been a big hit." Nancy grinned. "Last time I looked, more than a dozen people had bid on it."

"Good. Well, we're going to browse." Maddie and Lillian ventured toward a table of books.

"I wish Sam could see how everyone has pitched in to help," Joyce murmured. "Between their donations and purchases…." Sam had reluctantly agreed to have her parents stay until the day of the operation so they could see for themselves that she survived the procedure. Provided there was enough money for the surgery.

Nancy straightened a sign. "Bret told me that she had to go back to the hospital."

"For pain management," Joyce explained. "The

stress of the setback, fearing the second surgery—it's been increasing her pain. But she's home now. Luckily, J.C. says he can schedule the operation within a few days."

"We'll raise the money," Nancy encouraged.

Joyce smiled tremulously. "If we're short, we'll mortgage the house. But Sam can't know."

Ed stopped in front of them, letting the dolly he was pushing rest. "Matt Whitaker just dropped off this armoire for the sale."

"Oh my!" Joyce's hand flew to her mouth. "But he's already given us those beautiful cabinets."

"That's definitely a silent auction item!" Nancy exclaimed. "I'm going to ask Janie to put it on the Internet right away—let out-of-town dealers bid online or by phone." She rushed off to find her daughter.

Struck by the generosity of friends and neighbors, Joyce and Ed didn't see their own daughter until Bret pushed her wheelchair within a few feet of them.

"Sam!" Joyce exclaimed. "You're supposed to be home resting."

"And miss this?" Bret caught Ed's gaze, trying to convey the need not to overreact.

"Glad you feel well enough, punkin." Ed winked, disguising his concern.

"I thought it was going to be something like a yard sale," Samantha said in a small voice.

"Rosewood style," Ed replied. "Now, I've got to get this armoire in place. Joyce, you want to give me a hand?"

Joyce clearly wanted to stay and talk to Sam, but she relented, following her husband.

"Bret?" Sam asked.

He leaned down so he could hear. "Yep?"

"Why didn't you tell me how much work your family has done getting this thing organized and set up and—"

"You wanted something else to stress over?" He smiled to take the sting out of the words. "This is Mom's idea of fun. Not to mention Janie."

"I just can't believe all these people showed up."

"People you grew up knowing," he reminded her, his face close to hers. So close he wanted to touch her cheek, revisit their kiss.

She clutched his hand, pressing it tightly. "Bret…"

When she didn't finish her sentence, he met her gaze. "Remember, Sam. Close your mind to all the what-ifs. Your roots are here; they've just become rusty. But it doesn't have to stay that way." The curve of her neck beckoned him to smooth back her soft hair. But that would only tempt his memories. Of a kiss shared…now probably forgotten.

Hospitals had never been one of Bret's favorite places. He was used to them from all the times he'd visited his father. Heart surgery, by its nature, was a long, grueling process. He and his mother had nearly paced the finish off the waiting room floors, while younger Janie would usually fall asleep in a chair or on a couch. Maybe because of all those times, he hated waiting rooms, waiting for news that might be bad. But Bret knew he needed to appear calm and confident for the Shaws.

To his surprise, Sam had been uncharacteristically quiet in the days before surgery, seeming almost worn down, as though she'd given up. Still, she had been fervent in expressing her gratitude to his parents and the townspeople for raising enough money for the operation. Thinking of her oddly shifting behavior, he frowned.

"Something wrong?" Ed stared at him in worry.

Bret fumbled for something to distract the older man. "Just thinking about the horses Sam and I rode. Hoping for a mild winter so that when she's well enough, we can ride again."

A portion of Ed's obvious worry dissipated. "That was inspired—the horseback riding. Sam told her mother she felt like she was moving on her own, first time since the accident."

Bret shrugged. "Lucked onto a good idea."

Rachel, in hearing distance, snorted. "Only took him weeks to set it up. Even had me hide all her sweats so she'd have to wear jeans."

Nodding, Ed patted Bret's shoulder. "We feel safer knowing you've been here for Sam."

"Just part of the group effort. Rachel volunteers every spare minute she has." He gestured to Don and Trudy. "The whole family gives her incredible emotional support."

A knowing look entered Ed's eyes.

Joyce laid down the knitting she hadn't touched in more than an hour. "How much longer do you suppose it will take?"

"As long as it takes," Ed replied quietly. "She's in good hands. I feel better knowing J.C.'s operating than I did with that fancy doctor in New York."

Joyce laid her head against Ed's shoulder. "I wish I could take this pain for her."

Bret and Rachel tactfully looked away as Joyce wept.

"I can't bear to think how Sam will respond if this doesn't work," Rachel whispered.

"We agreed," Bret reminded her. "Only positive thinking. And prayers."

"Everyone in church…well, practically the entire town is praying for her." Rachel smiled shakily. "That's quite a chorus."

J.C. finally emerged from behind the forbidding, automatic double doors that led to surgery.

They stood as one. A tense, six-person lineup.

J.C. pulled off his surgical cap. His face was neutral.

From experience? Bret wondered. So relatives wouldn't fly into a panic?

"It went well," J.C. began. "The positioning of the fragment was more difficult than I anticipated. Still, we were able to remove it and also repair the herniated disks." He paused.

Joyce couldn't stay silent. "Will she be able to walk?"

"She didn't walk before the operation," J.C. reminded her. "Yes, she had some positive results in therapy, but they weren't yet long-term. Sam's going to have an extensive recovery period. Coupled with the time she's already lost from therapy, she'll be back at the beginning."

"But no complications?" Joyce asked. "She won't be paralyzed?"

"The next forty-eight hours will tell. But I don't anticipate complications. Why don't you all go home, get some rest?"

Ed shook J.C.'s hand as the others insisted they weren't budging, a noisy, incoherent refrain of refusals.

"When can we see her?" Joyce asked anxiously.

"I'll let you know when Sam's out of recovery," J.C. assured them. "She'll be fuzzy, but you can see for yourselves that she's all right."

Pumping J.C.'s hand, Ed nodded, his Adam's apple wobbling.

Bret couldn't imagine how the Shaws were going to leave so soon after Sam's surgery. Then again, Sam no longer had any leverage. The operation was over. And if her parents decided to stay a few more days, there wasn't anything she could do about it.

Plus, he suspected their presence would be good for Samantha, whether she admitted it or not.

Rachel patted his arm. "Relax, Rocky."

Bret glanced down, not realizing his fists were clenched.

"It's okay," she continued. "We're all just about over the edge. I don't think I've had a day this long since her last operation. Which was worse because I was here and she was in New York."

Diverting her attention, he nodded toward Joyce and Ed. "You think they're really going to leave?"

"Sure." Rachel smiled. "Just as soon as they know the outcome of Sam's surgery. I'm guessing that'll take at least four or five days."

Actually, it took two and a half. To everyone's relief, Sam felt the light pricks to her toes and feet. Delight ensued when she moved her toes a minuscule amount.

Ed, Joyce and Trudy were reduced to tears. Don beamed. And Rachel whooped.

Bret stood back, letting the family share the moment. Samantha was still too medicated to realize her parents had stayed longer than expected. Knowing it wouldn't be long before she was fully alert, the Shaws reluctantly made their plane reservations.

They were right, of course.

A day later, Sam was wide awake and demanding answers. "You told me you'd go back as soon as you knew I made it through surgery."

"Not exactly," Joyce corrected, smoothing Sam's dark hair. "We said we'd leave when we knew you were all right."

"Semantics."

Joyce smiled. "Now I know you're getting better. Glad you can kick up a fuss."

Samantha didn't remind her mother that she couldn't even kick her toes.

"And we'll be gone within the week," Joyce assured her.

Gripping the mattress, Sam tried to push herself up. "Oh, no. That wasn't our deal."

"Honey—" Joyce began.

"Nope. I made it through the surgery and I'm not paralyzed. No blood clots. No complications. Now you have to keep your end of the deal."

"It's only a short—"

Sam shook her head as emphatically as possible, considering all the machines she was hooked up to. "That was our deal."

Ed slipped his arm around Joyce's waist. "She's as stubborn as we are, my dear. Looks like we'd better move up those reservations."

"But—"

"We *did* promise. Not that I want to leave any more than you do. But Sam's a big girl." He smiled gently at his daughter, his eyes misting. "Even though she'll always be our little girl."

Sam swallowed. "Thanks, Dad. Mom."

Joyce sighed. "We all want our children to grow up to be independent. We just don't expect you to fly so high and strong on your own."

Ed leaned over and kissed Sam's cheek. "And you're as independent as they come."

Impulsively, she grabbed his hand. "Never too independent not to need you guys."

Mindful of all the tubes and wires, he gently hugged her. Unchecked tears flowing down her face, Joyce followed.

"I'll miss you both," Sam assured them, forcing

herself not to cry. "But I'll get well faster knowing what you're doing for Andy's kids."

Ed squeezed her hand. "He would be so proud of you, honey."

Sam nearly came undone. Andy was the one they'd all been proud of. He had always volunteered, done for others, cared more about everyone than himself. When they'd lost him, she'd always felt her parents had lost the most important part of themselves.

"The family's promised to watch out for you," Joyce added. "And we know the Lord always has you in His care. But don't forget. We're just a phone call away."

Ed smiled. "And a few continents."

Herb unloaded a new carton of wreaths and stacked them on a display just outside the front door of the nursery. Holiday merchandise had been arriving for awhile and with the living trees now prominently displayed, it was beginning to look a lot like Christmas. Along with poinsettias, mistletoe and fresh pine garlands, the place smelled as good as it looked.

The Conway family had pitched in to help put up decorations not only on Main Street, but also in the nursery. The business had to look especially good since holiday sales needed to carry them through the slow winter months until spring.

The living Christmas trees weren't flying out the door, but young people were more receptive to the idea. Bret helped one young family choose just the right tree. He rang up the purchase. "Sure you don't need any help setting it up?"

The husband shook his head. "We can handle it."

Bret handed him one of the wreaths that had just come in. "On the house."

Their little boy, who looked to be about four, grabbed the wreath, wagging it across the floor.

Bret smiled, then looked around for Peter, who was supposed to help customers load their trees. Not seeing him, Bret grabbed a flatbed dolly to retrieve the tree.

"Herb, will you watch the register?"

By the time Bret got back inside, Herb was finishing up with the wreaths. "Where's Peter?"

Herb shrugged his head toward the back.

Bret waited until the last customer left, then turned the *Open* sign around. "Herb, you still okay with Janie helping out until Christmas?"

"Sure. Your mom offered to watch the kids." He glanced toward the back where Peter was still dawdling. "D-day?"

"Getting close. Best thing I can say about him is that he's staying out of the way. I'm going to cut his hours, then wait until after Christmas to let him go."

"You going soft?"

"Maybe. I keep thinking there's something else wrong with him, besides being a slacker. Either way, I don't feel right about firing someone at Christmas."

Herb shook his head. "The guy's an encyclopedia on plants. Shame."

Bret glanced at his watch, realizing he was late

picking up Sam from therapy. Rachel had dropped her off, but he had agreed to take Sam home. The hours had slipped by between the extra work setting up for Christmas sales and staying longer than usual with his dad. "Can you close up?"

"Sure. Janie promised the kids they could make pizza so I'm in no hurry. Last time, I couldn't recognize half the toppings, but the M&M's were a little much for me."

Despite everything on his mind, Bret chuckled. "Wonder what she was thinking when she decided letting the kids pick the toppings was a good idea?"

Herb flattened the cardboard box. "Thinking? Uh-uh. No thinking going on there. Not with that idea."

J.C. had predicted that Samantha's progress would be slow but steady. Sam defied his predictions. Although the setback was difficult for her emotionally, she dug into her recovery like a woman possessed. During the weeks it had taken for the exterior surgical incisions to heal, she stretched daily, safe but consistent exercises in hopes of staying toned.

Again she underwent cervical traction and the electrode treatment that caused her muscles to contract. As soon as the incisions were healed, she was back in the pool. And when physical therapy started, she persevered with the core training until she could easily move her torso.

Bret, along with her family, had worried that Sam

might never take another step. But she had tackled every assignment as though her very life depended on it.

In ways, Bret suspected it did. Because Sam couldn't be Sam if she had to lean on anyone else. Her mind-set seemed to have spun back in time eight years. He felt that once she could move under her own power, Sam would wing her way back east, forgetting her connections to Rosewood. Forgetting him.

Harold finished Sam's session of leg stretches just as Bret arrived. "We can head over to the dressing rooms. Wanda should be through in a couple of minutes." Harold glanced up, seeing the next patient who was waiting for her session.

"I'll help Sam over to the dressing room," Bret offered, pushing her wheelchair forward.

Samantha didn't meet his eyes as she looped her arms around his neck. He savored the brief contact as he lifted her from the exercise table to the wheelchair. She reached for the wheels.

Bret stilled her hands. "Just a minute." He pulled a pair of fitted sport gloves from his jacket pocket and handed them to her. "You won't need these for long, but they'll protect your hands while you're using the chair. Should have thought of getting some before."

Sam held them motionlessly for a few moments, then touched the soft calfskin. "Thank you." Her voice was low.

"Rate you're progressing, you'll be out of the wheelchair in no time. Harold says he's never seen anything like it."

Her eyes remained downcast, staring at the gloves as though they were fascinating beyond description. "I've already been too big a bother."

Bret frowned at this attitude change, then knelt down to face her. "To who?"

She shrugged, still not meeting his eyes. "Everybody."

"Has *everybody* told you that?"

"I don't need to be told."

Bret battled his own need to take her hands, to confess he wanted nothing more than to be there for her, to give her anything and everything she might want. Instead he fell back on what he knew she would respond to. "Well, that's one way to get out of helping."

She finally met his eyes. "Get out of what?"

"Working on the magnolia. When you said you didn't want to, I thought you were just giving me a hard time. Guess you really meant it. You haven't even told me what the lab said."

"The *lab*? You may not have noticed, but I've been a little busy. Surgery, recovery, therapy—"

"Oh, please. That got you out of finishing the holiday decorations."

"You are the most exasperating man, Bret Conway!"

"And you're the easiest woman in the world to deal with?" He rose and grabbed the handles, pushing her wheelchair toward the dressing rooms.

Sam craned her head, unwilling to let him have the last word. "You know I never agreed to help with the stupid decorations. You dragged me downtown without even telling me why we were going. Come to think of it, why would you think I know anything about Christmas decorations? I don't even put up a wreath for the holidays! As for the magnolia, I *did* go to the park! Besides, it's winter! And…"

Wanda waited on the bench outside the ladies' dressing room, her face alight with mild curiosity.

Samantha shot him a look loaded with recognizable fury.

Hiding his amusement, Bret headed to the men's locker room to change.

Several minutes later, Sam emerged from the dressing room. Recognizing her patient's embarrassment, Wanda had gone on ahead. Sam left the new gloves in the locker with her clothes. Although they would have come in handy for strangling Bret and not leaving prints. Taking a deep breath, she looked around for him.

He lounged against a pillar, looking far too handsome. Couldn't he have aged badly? Become paunchy, bald, scruffy? Instead, he remained tall, lean, with a shock of thick hair that begged to be touched. So attractive she could melt. What was wrong with the women in Rosewood? He ought to be married with several children hanging from each limb.

Bret turned toward her just then. All six-plus feet of him. Six completely single, childless feet. She sighed. Doomed. She was doomed.

Had his shoulders been so broad when they were dating? His arms so sculpted? Self-consciously, she scrunched in her thin arms and tried to cover her even thinner legs. It wasn't fair that he'd gotten better while she'd deteriorated.

She reached for the wheels, but Bret's long strides closed the distance in seconds. He pulled her chair to one side and set the brakes. Even though she knew his intention, Sam caught her breath when he deftly picked her up, cradling her close. She wondered how it would feel to remain in his arms for something other than a utilitarian purpose. For him to simply hold her.

But his hold wasn't personal. No, she was his good deed. The pity case. Feeling like the proverbial sack of potatoes, she edged a touch closer as he walked down the ramp and the water lapped up over their legs, reaching waist level. The water was warm, intended to be soothing. But being in Bret's arms wasn't soothing. She felt anything but soothed. Instead, everything inside her stood on alert.

"You okay?"

It took a moment for Sam to realize Bret was speaking to her. "What?"

"You're hanging on pretty tight."

Realizing she was digging into his neck, Sam released her deathlike grip. "Sorry."

"No problem. I'm not going to let go until you're feeling safe."

She always felt safe in his arms. Not soothed, but safe. It didn't make sense, but Sam knew somehow it was right. That in his arms, she was where she belonged. Why had it taken her eight long years to find that out?

Wanda started the class. "Let's begin with a leg stretch."

Bret placed his hands around Sam's waist so that she could kick in a standing position. She couldn't thrust her feet very far yet. Despite knowing he saw her as an object of pity, she didn't want to move too far from Bret's hold. So she kept trying, even when the other members of the class stopped.

For the next exercise, Sam had to float, with Bret's assistance. He supported her abdomen while she attempted to move her legs in the water. The stretches helped; she'd retained some of the tone she had built during therapy.

Bret placed his hands around her waist for the next exercise and she forgot all about toning. Instead, she lingered as she leaned back against him, wishing they could be in each other's arms not to exercise, but because of their feelings.

Both their feelings.

Chapter Sixteen

❧

"No party this time," Sam grunted, as she hefted one foot in front of the other on the parallel bars.

Rachel jumped up and down as she clapped. "Whoo hoo! You're a party all by yourself! I knew you could do it. I just didn't know you could do it this fast! You could qualify for Olympic therapy! If there was Olympic therapy." Grinning ear to ear, Rachel clapped even harder.

Shaking her head, Sam couldn't suppress a smile of her own.

"At this rate, you'll be trying out crutches fairly soon," Harold encouraged.

"Did you hear that, Sam?" Rachel jumped up again.

A little embarrassed to have her own personal cheerleader, Sam nodded.

"Wait 'til your parents hear!"

"I imagine they can," Sam muttered.

Rachel waved her hand dismissively. "Oh, you."

Sam ignored the trickle of sweat that ran down her chest and the aching in her muscles. She was determined to get past this setback. Because when she was physically weak, she was emotionally vulnerable. How else could she explain her obsession with Bret and how he made her feel?

"You'll start with metal forearm crutches," Harold explained. "They give more support than traditional crutches."

"By Christmas?" Samantha asked.

"That's probably a little premature." Harold adjusted one of the bars. "But you're doing extremely well. And I've told you before—you don't mark your progress on a calendar. Some people take longer to make those first steps, then practically vault into crutches. Others go at a steady rate through each process. There's no average."

Rachel smiled more gently this time. "You goof. We're not all clones."

"Thank you, oh wise one."

"Any time. You getting tired?"

Exhausted. "I appreciate the support, but it's Harold's job to tell me when to stop."

"Stop." Harold smiled to take the edge off his command. "Your cousin's gotten well attuned to these sessions. Just soak today. No aqua exercises." He glanced at Rachel for confirmation.

At times Samantha felt about ten years old. Knowing they were only concerned about her, she dialed back her frustration. "Thanks, Harold. I wouldn't have gotten this far without you."

His round, ruddy face eased into a pleased grin. "You're a hard worker, Sam." He helped her into the wheelchair.

Even though she was exhausted, Sam was able to assist with the process. The dream of being able to leave the chair behind for good might actually be a possibility. By the time they had soaked, changed into dry clothes, and driven home, Samantha felt as though she'd run a marathon. The irony didn't escape her and she smiled weakly as Rachel pulled into the driveway.

Until she saw Bret's SUV. "What's he doing here?"

Rachel frowned. "That's not very gracious."

"I didn't mean it that way. I'm just really tired, and…." And she was being ungracious. Because she hated being the object of Bret's pity. Especially when she continued to find it more and more difficult to keep him out of her thoughts…and certainly her emotions.

He stood up just then, dusting off his knees. Seeing a pile of withered vines and leaves, she realized he'd been cleaning out the front flower beds.

"Looks like he's helping you out again." Rachel stated the obvious with a certain smack of satisfaction.

Shading his eyes from the setting sun, Bret recognized the car and headed toward them, knocking the dirt from his hands. The wind was whipping up, delivering the first threads of a winter storm.

Rachel hung back, allowing Bret to help Samantha into her wheelchair.

Once again, Sam melted under his touch, but she forced herself not to hang on to him overly long.

"How'd it go today?"

"Good," Sam murmured.

"Good?" Rachel repeated. "Fantastic. Sam's taking steps again."

"Wow. That was fast." Bret caught her gaze. "All your hard work's paying off."

"Speaking of hard work." Sam gestured to the flower beds. "You don't have to do my yard work."

"Just something to do while I was waiting. I figured you'd be through with your session about now. We got the results on the magnolia back from the lab so I brought them over."

Curiosity pushed aside much of her fatigue. "What'd they say?"

"The envelope's addressed to you."

She craned her head back to look at him. "And you didn't open it?"

"Nope."

"It's a lab report, not a love letter." She clapped her hand over her mouth as soon as the words were out. Of all the things she could have said….

Bret pushed her up the walk, then the ramp, pausing to pick up the envelope from the small table on the porch. "Did you lock the door?"

"No," she replied in a tiny voice, still cringing from embarrassment.

"Unless you'd rather stay outside?"

It was chilly, the wind making the late afternoon seem even colder. "No. You should've gone on in yourself."

"You weren't home."

Sam swallowed. Always a gentleman.

"I'm going!" Rachel hollered. "I've got to get over to Barton's before they close."

It was dim inside the house. Not very welcoming. Unconsciously, Sam shivered after she removed her jacket.

"Want me to turn on some lights?" Bret offered.

Samantha rubbed her arms. "Sure. Didn't know it was supposed to get this cold."

"Wind's coming from the north." He looked around. "Would you like a fire?"

"Oh, that's sounds wonderful."

Bret collected kindling and wood, efficiently building a small fire, getting the single log going without any trouble. The initial burst of flames quashed the pallor of the season's first storm. "I can add more logs later if you want to stay in here for a few hours. Otherwise, this one will last long enough to get you warmed up."

"Perfect," she murmured. "What is it about a fire in winter?"

"Reassurance. That light's always there, even when it doesn't seem likely."

Sam looked at him more closely. He wasn't prone to philosophy, but she didn't question him.

"I could use something warm to drink. Want me to see what I can rustle up?" Bret continued.

"Sure. Maddie made me some hot cider mix. I haven't tried it yet, but everything else she's made has been delicious." Sam trailed him into the kitchen and pointed to the counter. "It's in that apple-shaped jar.

She gave me an electric tea kettle, too, after she heard how the fire started. Said I shouldn't have that kind of problem with this one…" Her voice trailed off as she realized without that fire she might not have reconnected with Bret. Surreptitiously, she glanced sideways at him.

He filled the tea kettle, then paused. Had the thought occurred to him as well?

A cell phone rang suddenly, shattering the moment.

Sam was so entrenched in her thoughts, she didn't recognize whether the phone was her own or Bret's.

It rang again and Bret reached into his pocket, clearing his throat. "Hello." He listened, then ran a hand over his forehead. "I completely forgot. I'm over at Sam's. Yeah. I'll ask." He clicked the phone off, then exhaled. "I'm supposed to be at my parents' house for dinner. They'd like me to bring you."

She glanced down at her sweats. "I'm not dressed for—"

"It's casual," he interrupted, his eyes still dark with unspoken thoughts. "Sort of a tradition. It gets so crazy around Christmas that my mom always makes a simple midweek dinner so we can all get together and just visit since the weekends are always packed. Then we go see the live nativity."

"So they still do that…" Most of Rosewood's traditions had endured, despite some of the less pleasant changes in the rest of the world. She frowned. "What about the fire you built?"

"I can bank it." Leaving the kitchen, he picked up

the tongs that were part of the fireplace tool set, and hooked the log. Then he placed it in a cast-iron bucket on the stone hearth. "I'll douse it outside." First, he used the poker to carefully bank the remaining kindling. "Don't want another house fire."

Again their eyes met.

Sam wished she could read beyond the mahogany depths.

Tabby jumped in her lap, startling her. "Where have you been hiding?"

Bret reached for the bucket. "I didn't see her when we came in."

Petting the kitten, Sam watched him go outside. "Being discreet, were you?"

Tabby meowed and rubbed her head against Sam's hand. The kitten had stayed with Maddie during Sam's hospital stay and had apparently gained some independence. "Guess everything grows up and away."

"Ready?"

Sam jerked her head, not having heard him return. "I just need my jacket."

He took it from a low hook in the hall he'd installed for her use.

The sun now completely gone, the wind had gained an additional bite. The Blazer was warm inside, but quiet. Sam felt awkward, unsure. "I hope your mother didn't think she had to invite me."

"She's kind, but strong. She's had to be. So she doesn't do much she doesn't want to."

It wasn't exactly the answer Sam hoped for. She

drew herself farther toward the door. Bret's convivial mood had vanished. Feeling like the worst of fifth wheels, Sam wished she'd refused the invitation.

His parents were welcoming, though. Nancy leaned over for a hug.

"Hug implied," Robert told her with a genuine smile. "I have some sort of cold that I doubt you want."

"Those are so miserable," Samantha empathized. She'd been at more risk herself since the accident. And she knew that Robert's immune system was perilous.

"Annoying," he replied.

Nancy glanced at her husband, unable to disguise her worry. "He's had a sore throat for weeks now. And do you think he'll see the doctor?"

Bret turned to him, frowning. "Dad?"

"You know how much she worries. If I ran to the doctor every time I have a cough or sore throat I'd live at his office. Now, didn't I hear something about chicken pot pie?"

"Very un-Christmasy," Nancy explained. "We have plenty of traditional dishes for the big day, but we make this dinner a break from all the seasonal stuff. Every year we have something different—chili dogs, pizza, soup, something easy. This year it's chicken pot pie."

Janie and Herb stood in the kitchen while their children ran underfoot. Nancy seemed unperturbed by the distractions.

As usual, Sam felt useless since she couldn't offer to help.

Nancy turned to her. "Sam, could you do me a

favor? Keep Robert and Bret out of the kitchen?" Raising her eyebrows, she tilted her head in Herb's direction. "Already have enough help."

Sam agreed and rolled toward the family room, pausing at the entry.

"How are the orchids?" Bret asked.

Robert shrugged. "All right."

"Just all right? Maybe you do need to see the doctor."

"Don't you start, son. It's the time of year. More to do than tend the orchids."

"Do you still want me to take the white ones to church for Christmas Eve service?"

Robert nodded. "You did a nice job with the greenery and the poinsettias."

"But the orchids are extraordinary. Always makes me think of the special gifts for the Christ child."

Frozen in place, Sam listened shamelessly. When had she last thought of the holiday in terms of the Lord? Truly, truly thought in those terms. If she were honest, it had been well before Andy's death. She had wandered from the roots of her faith after she left Rosewood. Despite everyone's assurances, she'd wandered so far, she hadn't a clue how to return.

Chapter Seventeen

Despite the approaching storm, a crowd gathered at the live nativity, lifting their voices in song.

> Silent night, holy night
> Shepherds quake at the sight
> Glories stream from heaven afar
> Heavenly hosts sing Alleluia!
> Christ, the Savior is born, Christ the Savior is born.

It had always been Bret's favorite Christmas hymn. One that everyone seemed to know, even if only to hum. Voices combined, rising to trembling high notes, lingering over the most familiar words.

The participants in the live nativity seemed impervious to the cold. Strangely, it didn't seem as cold as it had earlier. Was it the warmth of the crowd? The protection of trees and shrubs that blocked some of the wind? Or just the feelings the enactment evoked?

Even his niece and nephews were quiet, leaning against their parents. A large star, that matched the one on Main Street, hung high in the tree behind the wooden stable that was just large enough to hold Mary, Joseph and the crèche. A few cows and sheep flanked each side.

Bret had been surprised when Sam agreed to come along. Especially after he'd overheard her remark. *Guess everything grows up and away.* And he'd hoped she might have changed. Glutton for punishment, he was. Once a wanderer, always a wanderer.

Robert coughed suddenly, a deep, guttural cough that didn't sound good. What if it wasn't just a cold? Bret was already worried about how pale and fatigued his dad had been looking.

Bret leaned over to the right. "Mom?"

Janie elbowed him sharply, singing louder to shush him.

He could ask later.

Sam looked around and up at him in question. He mouthed the words of the hymn until she faced forward again.

His mother glanced over at him in question. The rule in their house had always been that all differences were to be resolved before Christmas Day.

Yes, they would definitely be talking.

Sam rubbed her hands together. Sitting, rather than moving around, she must be cold. His irritation slowly faded. Sam couldn't help being who she was any more than he could prevent his feelings for her. He leaned down so that he could whisper. "Are you about ready to go home?"

"Only when you are. The carols are…nice."

He remembered the old quilt he kept in the back of the Blazer for soccer games and picnics. Wouldn't take a minute to get it out. It was easy to weave through the people, retrieve the quilt. Kneeling down, he smoothed the old patchwork piece over Samantha's lap.

"You didn't have to get this," she whispered, her breath warm against his cheek.

Bret wished he could remain by her side, reignite the love they had shared, garner a promise for the future.

She leaned back.

Knowing that wasn't going to happen, he rose and stood behind her chair. And glanced at the star hung in the tree. The star that symbolized new life, new promise. One that wasn't in his future. Not with Samantha.

Christmas Eve day should have been uneventful. Instead, the doorbell started ringing around nine in the morning. Neighbors bringing over little gifts. Cookies, fudge, handmade potholders, gloves, a calendar, jams. Samantha felt terrible that she hadn't remembered the custom and didn't have any gifts to reciprocate with. But everyone assured her they didn't expect anything.

Maddie stopped by with a deep-blue, hand-knitted shawl. "I made it so that it'll work now, wrapping around you in the chair, but it'll transition with you when you're walking again."

"I love it!" Samantha stroked the soft yarn. She pivoted, reaching for one of the few gifts she had purchased. "I didn't make this, but I hope you'll enjoy it."

"You didn't have to get me anything."

Sam snorted delicately. "Why do people say that?"

Maddie laughed. "I don't know. Actually, I love presents." She unwrapped the bulky packaging and lifted out a hand-carved candle. "Oh my!"

"It's lemon verbena. If you'll look inside, there's a little bottle with the same essential oil so you can freshen the wick."

Maddie put the candle to her nose and inhaled deeply. "It's so unusual...and comforting, somehow."

"Had a lot of time on my hands." Samantha smiled. "So I did some research on Rachel's laptop. I know about lavender, but this one's supposed to have similar properties."

"I don't remember ever seeing this combination before."

"I ordered it," Samantha confessed. "It's not too common."

"Which makes me like it even better. I wonder how it would be as a tea," Maddie mused.

Samantha laughed. "I'll let you figure out that one."

"Well, I'd better get back to Mom."

"Wait." Sam pivoted again, retrieving a small package. "This one's for her."

"Oh, Sam! You really didn't have to!" Maddie sounded distressed. "She won't remember you gave it to her."

"That's not why I bought it," Sam reassured her. "Rachel took me downtown one day. I saw an old-fashioned brooch in the window of the antique store and thought of your mother. I hope she likes it."

Maddie clutched the package tightly. "I know she will. This is so…" She swallowed. "So thoughtful."

Samantha patted the new shawl. "So is this."

Maddie laughed. "Will you be here tomorrow?"

"Ah, Rachel intends to kidnap me for family festivities. What about you?"

"We've been invited to dinner with some of Mom's old friends."

The doorbell rang.

"That's my cue." Maddie pointed to the back door. "I'll go out that way."

Samantha opened the front door.

Rachel stood on the porch, stomping her feet. "It's getting cold."

"Then come inside."

Rachel did.

"You can take your coat off."

"Nope." Rachel rocked on her heels. "I've come to collect you."

"Collect me?"

"Yep. And don't even try saying no unless you want the reinforcements over here."

Sam saw the writing on the wall. "Your mom and dad?"

Rachel nodded. "My orders are to bring you home. Between you and me, surrender is your best option."

"Is your mom making a ham?"

"I think so."

"Okay. I surrender."

"Nice shawl," Rachel commented. "Emphasizes the color of your eyes."

"Thanks. Maddie made it."

"Wow. Hope you're not expecting anything handmade from me."

"Not since the time you made me a mug out of salt dough. Nearly choked to death on my Kool-Aid."

"Let's grab your pajamas and a change of clothes."

"What?"

"Didn't I tell you?" Rachel headed toward the bedroom. "This is an overnight kidnapping. That way you get to spend Christmas Day with us."

Samantha rolled her eyes. "Good thing I keep my bag packed for therapy. I just have to add pajamas. Oh, and the gifts on the table there."

Rachel picked through the closet. "On the positive side, Mom's making French toast for breakfast."

Sam hadn't been looking forward to spending Christmas Eve alone, so she didn't have to be coerced. "We'll have to bring Tabby."

Rachel sighed as she reached for the kitten's bed. "I guess I should be glad you didn't bring home that horse you rode."

Samantha's aunt and uncle were full of grins and hugs when she and Rachel arrived. All sorts of wonderful aromas were coming from the kitchen and Sam was glad she hadn't put up any resistance.

Despite the time difference, Samantha phoned her parents after dinner, wanting to share the special day, tell them about her progress at therapy. Rachel had videoed her steps and e-mailed the session. Ed and Joyce didn't have daily e-mail access, but they would see it on their weekly visit to the nearest bit of civilization, which was a combination general store, post office and fueling depot.

Sated, happy with her phone visit, Sam felt it had been a near perfect day. Then everyone started stirring. "What's up?"

"Candlelight service at church," Rachel replied as though Samantha had been informed of the plan.

"Oh no. You didn't—"

"Sam!" Trudy's face filled with distress. "It won't be the same if you don't come."

She intended to refuse. She opened her mouth to say no. However, the trio of pleading faces was more than Samantha could withstand. Still, she scrambled for an excuse. "I didn't bring anything to wear."

Rachel casually studied her nails. "I did."

The forage in the closet.

"Fine." It was only one time.

Rosewood Community Church dated back to 1853, built from native stone by German pioneers. The intricate stained-glass windows were also the products of immigrant artisans.

The church had survived storms, even fire, and the tall spire had beckoned from the center of town since its first stone was laid.

Rows of smooth, well-worn wooden pews were nearly full; the organ played, all stops out, to herald the start of the service. As was the custom, they began by singing carols, many older than the building itself. The reverence of the sanctuary surrounded Samantha in a way that was both reassuring, yet now unfamiliar. She'd spent nearly every Sunday of her early life in this church. Glancing around, she recognized almost everyone in the congregation. All but those who had joined since she'd left Rosewood.

Turning her attention to the pulpit, Samantha spotted white orchids. Exquisitely perfect orchids. Nearly as beautiful as the holiday itself.

After opening remarks, the pastor read from the second chapter of Luke, the story of the Christ child's birth. Samantha listened to the words she'd heard many times before. Somehow, this time they seemed directed to her.

> And, lo, the angel of the Lord came upon them, and the glory of the Lord shone round about them: and they were sore afraid. And the angel said unto them, Fear not: for, behold, I bring you good tidings of great joy, which shall be to all people.

To *all* people.

The choir's rich blend of voices filled the sanctuary

as ushers at the end of each pew lit a candle. Then each person in turn lit the next candle until the entire church flickered with pinpoints of light. The overhead lights were dimmed. And the congregation joined in with the choir as they sang "Angels From the Realms of Glory."

The emptiness Samantha had felt for so long began to fill as she remembered what she'd been missing. What she needed and wanted again.

After the closing prayer, people blew out their candles as they quietly filed out. Sam reached for her wheels, when Bret appeared from out of nowhere.

"Let me."

He pushed the chair out through the hallway and into the crisp night. She looked around, but her family seemed to have melted into the crowd. Just as she was going to ask, he turned her chair so that she could look back toward the sanctuary. Trudy and Rachel were probably talking a mile a minute to friends while Don waited patiently.

Above them, the famous Texas sky was living up to its reputation. Broad and dark, it showcased the stars that shone as though polished for the specialness of this night.

"Would you like a ride home?" Bret asked. "I was going to stop by anyway."

His words warmed her, chasing away any chill in the temperature. "Well, actually, I'm staying with Don and Trudy. Rachel didn't really give me a choice."

"She can be pretty relentless."

"I'm sure it would be all right if you'd like to come

by. I know they've invited friends to come over after the service. And the wassail smells wonderful. Aunt Trudy wouldn't let us even sneak a taste."

He smiled. "A ride then?"

"Oh." It should be a little thing, but she literally came with a lot of baggage. Loading her in the car, stowing her chair. And then reversing the process when they arrived.

"Problem?"

"For you. The chair and all."

"I'll let you know when I'm too frail to lift it, okay?"

Despite the cold, his hands were warm as they lifted her out of the chair, his dark hair soft beneath her fingers as she hung on to his neck. "I forgot my gloves," she blurted, not wanting to let go.

His face only inches from hers, stilled. The white puffs of their breath mingled, at odds with the increasing warmth of their eyes. They were so close she could see golden flecks mixed in with the brown. Questions swirled in their depths. Then they dropped to her lips. Her gaze followed. She remembered his gentle touch, his promise of love.

This night of promise…

Their lips met, mingled. Samantha closed her eyes, feeling the thrill of his nearness.

"Samantha?" Trudy called out. "Are you riding home with Bret?"

She returned to earth with a jolt. Mixed signals flew about like snowflakes in a winter storm. One moment it seemed all Bret felt for her was pity, then…a horrible thought seized. Was this, too, a sign of his pity? Confused, she didn't answer her aunt.

Bret cleared his throat, his voice low. "I'm taking her. Shouldn't be long."

Trudy waved merrily. "See you there!"

After a tense, quiet ride, they reached the house. Don and Trudy weren't far behind. Rachel had chosen to ride with friends, who pulled up next, then spilled out of the car, laughing.

Bret's fingers grazed the sprig of mistletoe in his pocket, then crushed it. This wouldn't be the quiet setting he'd hoped for.

Don and Trudy Shaw's house, another old Victorian, was larger than Samantha's. Guests were scattered in the large entry hall that was a room unto itself, the kitchen and the receiving parlor.

"Any place special you want to light?" he asked once they were inside.

Sam seemed to have collected herself, no longer looking shaky. "I'd like to go to my room for a minute. Do you want to get some wassail and meet me in the back parlor?"

He thought for a moment. It had been awhile since he'd been in the house. "The room next to the conservatory?"

She nodded.

Bret greeted the others crowded in the kitchen. Skipping the spread of goodies, he balanced two cups of wassail as he edged back through the jostling bodies.

The back parlor was wonderfully quiet.

"I hope this isn't too grim," Samantha apologized as she wheeled inside. "There's a fire in the front room, but it's pretty crowded. Some of Aunt Trudy's friends are in the choir and they plan to sing carols by the piano. They won't stay long, but it's a little intense for me."

"Remember, my mother invites every stray in the land. Tomorrow's going to be a madhouse."

Sam glanced up, finally meeting his gaze. "It's been quite a year, hasn't it?"

"Especially for you."

She interlaced her fingers, a sure sign of nerves. "One thing about being in the hospital. It gave me a lot of time to think. And it occurred to me that I never thanked you. For saving me, I mean."

He waved away the words. "I wheeled you outside. Not exactly as though I climbed a ten-story building that was about to fall down."

"Still. Thank you." She paused. "And you've helped with so many other things. The kitchen would still be hunks of charred wood without you. That meant a lot to my parents…to me." Sam lifted the end of her shawl and pulled out a small package. "This isn't very much to say thank you, but it's a token of my gratitude. And to wish you a merry Christmas." Speech done, she watched him anxiously.

No pressure there. Carefully, he removed the silver ribbon and wrapping paper. The box came from the custom jeweler in town. What in the world? He removed the square of tissue. A perfect replica of Ranger stared back at him. Picking up the silver piece, he saw it could be used as a lapel pin or tie tack.

"Rachel arranged to have it made for me," Samantha explained in a rush. "We looked through all the photo albums until we found a picture of Ranger."

His horse. The one he'd had as a child until they could no longer afford to keep him.

"While I was in the hospital, Rachel carried through with the jeweler." Samantha explained. "You gave me the gift of freedom. I wanted you to know how much that meant…means to me."

It took a lot to choke him up. He'd grown up under the shadow of his father's poor health, the subsequent insecurity of the family business, and uncertain finances at home. Then the broken engagement. Still….

"This is special, Sam. Really special."

Her eyes seemed as large as twenty-carat jewels. "You really like it?"

"No. I love it."

The word reverberated between them, a taut line that could barely hold its own weight.

To break its spell, Bret reached into his pocket and withdrew a gift.

Impossibly, Samantha's eyes grew even larger when he gave it to her.

Hands trembling, she tugged off the ribbon, then the paper. It, too, was a jeweler's box. A thin, rectangular one. Curiosity played over her face as she opened it.

A silver chain with a small, engraved disk lay in the box. She lifted the chain, reading her name.

"Ankle bracelet," he explained. "For the next steps."

She clutched the bracelet in her hand. "And if I don't?"

"You will. There's never been one thing in your life you've wanted that you didn't get."

Samantha glanced down, not lessening her ferocious grasp on the bracelet. "That's what you think?"

"It's what I know, Sam." He wished it could be different, but there it was. He'd fallen for her again. And like a wounded bird, once healed, she would fly away again. This time for good.

Chapter Eighteen

Bret always hated taking down Christmas decorations. Not because it was a chore, but because it meant the season was over for another year. The season of hope.

Even though sales were slow, he didn't intend to ask Herb to leave. But it was time to deal with his other employee.

Stacking holiday cards they'd received from vendors, friends and neighbors, Bret paused when he heard Peter shuffle into the office. "Would you shut the door?"

"No point. Herb knows what's going on."

"I gave you longer than ninety days, Peter. You didn't even try."

"That all?"

"What are you going to do now?"

Peter shrugged.

"Why'd you give up on your job? Make it impossible for me to keep you on?"

"Right. You were planning to give my job to your brother-in-law all along."

Bret took an envelope from the middle drawer. "Here's your check."

Peter snatched the envelope.

"Herb wasn't planned." Bret stood. "I found out he'd been laid off the day before he started working here."

Mistrust and disbelief shrouded the other man's face. "You'd have found some reason."

Whatever motivated Peter was going to remain the man's secret. "Need your key, Peter."

He snorted, dug out his keys, then slipped off the one to the nursery. Ignoring Bret's outstretched hand, he tossed it on the desk.

After he left the office, Bret picked up the key, wondering for the first time since he'd worked in the business if they should change the locks. It was a sour thought, one he detested.

What a way to start the new year.

The forearm crutches were a challenge. Sam was beyond thrilled to finally leave the wheelchair, even though J.C. told her she would still need it until she was stronger. And then as a backup. Samantha wanted to walk all over town, up and down Main Street, through every street and into every business. In truth, she could only manage to get around her house.

So, when Bret asked if she wanted to go horseback riding again, she was excited. Despite the effects of winter, the Markham ranch remained welcoming. Still awkward, Sam felt a bit like the Tin Man in *The Wizard of Oz* as she lumbered inside the stable.

Bret, on the other hand, was decidedly casual about her movements, acting as though she was simply walking along normally. "You never did tell me how the tests came out on the magnolia."

She blinked. "I completely forgot about them. I don't even know what I did with the envelope."

"Huh."

"You just remembered *now*?"

He looked at her calmly. "You have a schedule for remembering things?"

"Of course not. It's just that…" Yes, it was just what? That she felt as though in a moment she might have to be hauled onto the horse like one of the old knights from the days of King Arthur?

"Yes?"

"Nothing. I just feel silly forgetting about it."

"Do you have your carrot?"

Remembering, she dug into her jacket pocket, then advanced toward Sugar. Mr. Markham had assured them that Sam could ride the same mount. It was probably her imagination, but Samantha thought the horse remembered her.

Once the chestnut mare was saddled, Bret helped her up onto the horse. The crutches were left leaning against the wall. Able now to nudge Sugar with her knees, Samantha felt a glorious burst of freedom.

This time, Bret didn't have to grab onto Sugar's halter or lead the mare. Sam truly was in control. Ears pricked up, Sugar pawed at the ground, ready to run. But Sam wasn't foolish enough to give the horse her head. Still early in her recovery, she wasn't going to risk another accident. There had been a time when she wouldn't have given a second thought to the danger. But that, too, was the old Samantha.

As they rode, Bret stayed on the flatter ranch ground. "I don't feel comfortable riding uphill just yet."

She nodded. "Wiser."

He looked surprised.

"What?"

"Nothing."

"What?" she insisted.

"I thought you'd want to try to do more."

"I always have, haven't I?"

"Forget it, Sam. I meant for this to be fun, not psychotherapy."

She inhaled deeply. "It is. Fun, I mean. I'm so grateful that I can walk again, even with the clunky crutches, and even only for a few steps at a time. But this…this is utter freedom. I feel like I could ride forever."

His expression was one she couldn't fathom.

"Bret?"

He shook his head. "Nothing. It's good to be out here. I'd like to have a horse of my own again. But…"

"What?"

"Nothing."

"Oh no. You didn't let me off the hook. What's stopping you from getting a horse?"

His laugh was humorless. "Can't afford it."

She immediately sobered. "Is it the business?"

"Got hit pretty hard by the recession."

"Why didn't you tell me?"

"You have enough to worry about."

Heartsick, she gazed at him. "And you don't? The business and your father…and you've been helping me, taking time away from work. Why didn't you let me know what was going on?"

"You never used to be concerned about everyday worries."

No, she hadn't. She'd flown through life as though everything should and did fall into place at her whim. How had she been so thoughtless?

The clink of halters melded with creaking saddle leather. The only other sounds were those of hooves clip-clopping on the hard winter ground.

The loud, unexpected ring of a cell phone seemed as alien as if a hovercraft had suddenly descended.

Bret reached into his jacket and quickly answered. "Mom?" As he listened, his face sobered. "I'll be there as soon as I can."

Sam felt her throat dry up. "What is it?"

"Dad's in the hospital."

"You go on back without me. I'll manage."

He looked at her as though she'd sprouted a second head. "We'll get to the hospital, but I'm not abandoning you out here."

"I can ride a little faster," she offered, increasing her pace. "Do you know what's wrong with him?"

"That sore throat and cough he had. Turns out it was

strep. Developed into bronchial pneumonia. Since his heart transplant, any infection's serious."

Worried, Samantha tried to hurry Sugar along. With the exception of Andy's horrific accident, Sam's own family had been blessed with good health, good fortune.

It had taken eight years for her to finally understand. When she'd asked Bret to choose between his family and their marriage, she had put him in an untenable position. It wasn't only that Bret had to run the family business. He'd been the one Nancy and Janie had leaned on. And Bret must have been terrified that he would lose his father.

They quickly reached the stable. Once Bret helped Samantha off Sugar, he grabbed her crutches.

"Bret, I can get a ride home—"

"I'll ask Butch to take care of the horses so we can leave now." He ran from the stable.

She made her way as quickly as possible to the Blazer.

Bret was back in time to open her door, stash her crutches in the rear and get her seated. Then he roared off, leaving a trail of dust.

By the time he reached the highway, Bret pulled out his cell phone again, dialing quickly. "Tucker? Bret. Need you to know I'm speeding on the highway. I'll slow down if I see another car." He paused, listening. "Yeah. It's my dad. We're on the way to the hospital. Thanks."

"Sounds like you've done that before," Sam ventured in a quiet voice.

"Tucker lets his deputies and the highway patrol know. Helps a lot."

She would have known that if she'd stayed around. Instead, Bret had handled it on his own, stepping up to shoulder his entire family's load.

Although Bret exceeded the speed limit, he didn't drive recklessly. Not meeting much oncoming traffic, it didn't take long to reach town. Since Bret had insisted on bringing along Sam's wheelchair in case it was needed, he pulled it out of the back.

Sam didn't complain, knowing it would be faster than if she tried to use her crutches. When they reached the emergency room, Nancy jumped up as soon as she spotted them.

"Dad?" Bret's voice was under control, but Sam heard the tension.

"He's stable. I knew he should have had that sore throat checked, but first it was the holidays. Then he insisted that his cough was going away."

Bret hugged her. "You'd have had more luck moving a brick wall. With all the staph infections he's had, he probably didn't think about strep."

Nancy reached down and squeezed Samantha's hand. "This is the last place you want to be. I'm sorry, dear."

Janie rushed into the waiting area, her hands filled with foam cups. "I only got two." From the worry on her face, it was clear she had much more on her mind than coffee.

"I can get more," Samantha offered, pointing to the cup holder and carryall attached to her chair. "I'd like to."

Bret met her eyes. "Thanks. That'd be great."

Accustomed to carrying everything she might need

in her pockets, Sam slipped on the gloves he'd given her and wheeled toward the vending machines. She was able to set the brake, and stand to put the coins in. Funny. Felt as important as anything she'd ever done.

By the time she arrived back with a double-strength coffee for Bret, he sat beside his mother, giving her quiet support. Janie had stepped outside to use her cell phone.

"She's checking on the kids," Nancy explained. "They're with her neighbor until Herb gets home."

"How are *you* doing?"

Nancy smiled faintly. "I always worry too much and then Robert's okay."

From the sober looks on their faces, Samantha wondered if that could be true. She handed Nancy a package of mints she'd gotten out of the machine.

"Thank you. These will chase away that hospital coffee taste."

Not knowing what else to do, Sam folded her hands and waited.

When the doctor, a man Sam didn't recognize, entered the waiting room, Bret and his mother jumped up. Janie closed her cell phone and ran inside. Feeling their anxiety, Sam leaned forward in her wheelchair, straining to hear.

The doctor addressed Nancy. "That fellow of yours is stubborn. He should have come in sooner."

Sam swallowed a burst of dread.

"His kidney function is almost gone. We're putting him on dialysis."

Nancy cleared her throat. "Will…will they work again?"

Dr. Beak shook his head. "I don't know."

Janie's face crumpled. And Nancy buried her face in Bret's shoulder. In less than a day, Bret's world had turned upside down.

Samantha stayed at the hospital as long as she could, until she felt she would become a liability. Bret had snagged the doctor's attention and disappeared. Quietly, Sam phoned Rachel and asked for a ride home.

Soberly, Rachel offered the family her prayers and support, promising to phone the pastor as well. Belatedly, Samantha realized she hadn't even been able to offer that.

Feeling entirely superfluous, Sam was as silent as her house when she and Rachel came inside.

"The prayer chain's started," Rachel told her. "Won't take long to alert everyone." She put her keys in her pocket. "I forgot to ask if you'd eaten anything."

"Not hungry." Sam looked around blankly. Too exhausted to deal with the crutches, she'd retreated to her wheelchair. Strangely, it was comforting. Which was nothing less than ridiculous since she'd railed at it, despised it, wished it to self-destruct.

"Do you want me to stay over?"

"What?" Sam looked up. "No. Of course not. I'm not the one who's sick. But I am completely useless. Not one thing I can do."

"Yes, there is. Pray for Bret and his family."

Sam gripped her hands together. "I'm not sure I remember how."

"It'll come back to you." Rachel shivered. "It's kind of cold in here."

"I've been gone all day, haven't turned up the thermostat."

Rachel headed toward the hall. "I'll do that and make us some cocoa. Don't want you to turn into an icicle."

While Rachel rustled in the kitchen, Samantha remembered the evening Bret had built a fire for her. Funny how one person could seem to fill an entire room, change the tenor of the whole house. As she looked toward the empty fireplace, she noticed a large envelope on the hearth. The test results on the magnolia? Crossing the room, she picked up the envelope and saw that the return address was the laboratory's.

She reached over, flipping on the lamp. Samantha paused when she saw that the flap was still sealed. Ah, gentleman Bret. Reading the results, her surprise grew with each word. The bark mulch surrounding the magnolia contained ammonia sulfate—a weedkiller. And in huge proportion.

Rachel returned. "Furnace is turned up, water's boiling." She frowned. "Why do you look worse than when I left the room?"

"The lab report about the magnolia tree. There's weedkiller mixed in with the bark mulch. It's killing the tree."

Rachel frowned. "Mac wouldn't do that on

purpose." Just about everybody in town knew the park's caretaker, running into him during outings through the decades. The man lavished attention on the grounds as though it was his own personal estate.

"No. But someone must have," Samantha mused.

"Can you save the tree?"

"I'll need to phone a friend at the university where I lectured—back in New York." Sam scanned the rest of the page. "Leonard's an expert on trees, more so than me. It's his speciality—even does postmortems on them. Not that we want it to come to that with the magnolia. I do know that we'll have to remove all the contaminated bark, cleanse the roots, replace the soil…"

"We, kimosabe?"

"With Mac's help, of course. I can't bother Bret about it right now."

Rachel slowly acquiesced. "Well…yeah."

"Might be a nice surprise for Bret when his father…" Sam swallowed. "Gets well."

"Don't forget what I said. Prayer *does* help. You're living proof."

"Me?"

"You don't have any idea, do you? Your parents, my parents, me…everyone in church, we've been praying for you since you first had your accident. We haven't ever stopped."

Speechless, moved, Sam stared at her cousin.

"I'll go get our cocoa. And think about it, Sam. Prayer's just like your steps. One word at a time."

* * *

"How's he doing?" Sam asked quietly at the Conways' front door.

Nancy smiled. "You don't have to whisper, dear. Hello, Rachel. Come in, both of you. Robert will love the company. He's going stir-crazy inside. Insists he's well enough to get back to his orchids."

"Sounds like a good sign." Sam carefully navigated through the door with her crutches.

Nancy showed them into the family room. Robert was stretched out on the long leather couch.

Although he looked tired, his expression brightened. "Two pretty girls. That's good medicine."

Rachel grinned. "I definitely need to see you more often, Mr. Conway."

Nancy turned the television off. "As you can tell, he's still a rascal."

He snorted half-heartedly. "She's a worrywart."

Nancy sent him a mock look of reproof. "I've got hot cider. Any takers?"

"Sounds good," Sam replied.

"I'll help," Rachel offered, already rising.

Sam watched Robert as Nancy left the room. His eyes followed her every move. Sweet. After so many years…

He swiveled his head back, looking at her. "So, you're getting around like a sprinter, I see."

"Not quite yet, but it feels great to move under my own steam. You and your family organizing the fundraiser—I can't begin to say how much it means to me, how you've changed my life."

"That's all to Nancy."

Rachel walked in holding two mugs.

Nancy was only a few steps behind. "What is?"

"The fundraiser." Sam accepted a mug. "I was just saying how much it means to me. Not only all the money you raised, but that you worked so hard, and—"

"It was my privilege." Nancy glanced at her husband. "We've been involved in a lot of fundraisers over the years, but, this one, well, it was as though we were giving back."

Sam knew instantly what she meant.

"This cider is delicious," Rachel exclaimed. "Perfect for a winter day."

Sam appreciated her cousin's quick distraction.

"So, Mr. Conway, any idea how long it'll be before you can get back to your greenhouse?" Rachel asked.

"They don't tell me anything," he replied in an exaggerated whisper.

Nancy smiled as she shook her head at him. "Luckily, he's on in-home dialysis. So he won't get tired out spending hours at a facility. We're hoping that on the next visit, his doctor gives the okay for less bed rest."

"Then it'll be back to my beauties," Robert said with satisfaction. He winked at Nancy. "'Course, it's not bad being inside with my one beauty."

Nancy blushed. "As you can see, the medication's affecting his vision."

Sam sat back in the comfortable chair, watching their exchange. And wondering if she'd ever have anything that wonderful of her own.

* * *

Bret rocked back on his heels, allowing a handful of bark mulch from the magnolia to sift through his fingers. "Ammonium sulfate?"

"I'm afraid so. I kept this sample from the mulch we dug out around the tree," she explained. "Thought we might need it to figure out how the ammonia sulfate got into the bark."

"I know how it got there."

"You do?"

"This is the bark mulch we stock at the nursery."

"But you wouldn't put ammonium sulfate on a magnolia."

Bret dusted off his hands, remembering the anger on Peter's face, his subtle threats. "Not me."

"Herb?" she asked hesitantly.

"He hasn't worked on any outside jobs like the park."

"Then—"

"I can't say until I'm sure." He rose, picking up the sabotaged bark. "But that won't take long."

Peter lived in an old wreck of a mobile home. More rust than metal, the heap was parked far back on Val Gertenstal's land. The trailer's only redeeming feature was that it was hidden behind a thick copse of trees.

Bret looked for Peter's Camaro, but didn't see it.

"Lock the doors and don't get out," he instructed.

Worried, Sam grabbed his hand. "You don't think he'll…do something?"

"Doubt it. Cowards sabotage."

Bret walked up the rickety steps and knocked on the door. The place was silent. So silent Bret guessed there wasn't any electricity. No low hum from a heater or refrigerator, nothing.

Walking around the side of the trailer, Bret spotted a dented garbage can next to a pile of logs. As he walked closer, he saw another container, an old plastic tub. When he was near enough, he recognized the bark mulch. Compressing his lips into a tight line, he knelt down and scooped up some of the bark. White grains of ammonium sulfate were mixed liberally with the bark. From the corner of his eye, Bret spotted a printed sack. He pulled it toward him, recognizing the brand of bark he carried at the nursery. Flipping open his cell phone, Bret used it to take several photos of the mix and the spot where he'd found it. Then he scooped some of the contaminated bark back into its original bag.

The familiar sound of Peter's car approached. Bret gripped the bag and rounded the corner of the trailer.

Peter saw him, his face sagging into lines of shock.

"Ammonium sulfate? Why didn't you just take an axe and chop the tree down?"

"The tree's *your* responsibility. The Conway nursery's responsibility."

"You thought you were going to run me out of business? That people would decide we suddenly didn't know how to care for a tree?"

Angered, Peter twisted his frown into a near snarl. "You won't fix your own problems by making ones for me. But, in case you think it would be a good idea to try something else, I've got evidence." He held up the bag. "I've got pictures, Peter. And I'll take the whole lot to the sheriff if so much as one petunia is destroyed."

Sullenly, Peter stared at him, but didn't respond.

Disgusted with the man and his delinquent vandalism, Bret got into the Blazer and backed out quickly.

"Why'd he do it?" Sam questioned anxiously.

"Hoping to wreck the business."

"Bret!"

"This isn't going to do it." He drove up the dusty ground, turning onto the highway.

Sam exhaled. "Do you think he'll try again?"

"Not sure. I can't figure the guy out." Bret accelerated, wanting to put distance between themselves and Peter.

Sam was quiet for several minutes as he drove. When she spoke, it was softly. "Bret?"

He spared a glance away from the road.

She fiddled with the armrest. "I've been thinking about something. You can tell me it's a terrible idea. It's not as though I have any real business experience…well, I mean the retail kind, or actually anything like that. Mine was just me…" Her voice trailed off.

"Sam?"

"Yes?"

"Want to tell me what the idea is?"

Nervously, she swiped one hand across her forehead. "Well…it's something I've thought about before. Just not with me as the person doing it, you know? And you care so much about the environment and the loss of biodiversity. I mean, look at how you're raising live Christmas trees and specializing in native plants and—"

"Sam?"

She looked at him curiously.

"The idea?"

She exhaled again. "Developing sustainable food crops. Think of all the species we've already lost, plant and animal. And the crops are good for the community, to preserve the soil, cut down on chemical pesticides…" Sam paused for a breath. "And, maybe it could be another revenue for Conway's."

He was silent for a moment.

"You hate it."

"No. Wish I'd thought of it. I've been lost in tunnel vision with the nursery…wanting a lot of my dad's imprint to always be there."

Her beautiful eyes darkened in understanding. "It will, Bret. That won't ever change. Your dad's passed down everything good about himself to you."

Searching her gaze, he wondered if she really meant what she said. And if it was enough.

Chapter Nineteen

The magnolia was gradually responding to its nursing. Its fate wasn't certain, but Sam remained hopeful.

"Looks good," Bret praised.

Now proficient with her crutches, Sam walked in a semi-circle toward the rear of the tree. "It probably won't bloom for...well, I honestly don't know how long. But it's got a fifty/fifty chance of surviving."

"You really took over the project."

Samantha paused. "With your...workload, you didn't need to be worrying about the magnolia, too." Bret's father had never been removed from dialysis; his kidney function was now gone permanently.

"Dad will be okay."

Sam wasn't sure if he was assuring her or himself. "Of course he will." She couldn't imagine the kind, charming man not recovering. "People can stay on dialysis indefinitely, can't they?"

"Depends. Every case is different. Dad's is more

complicated because he's already an organ recipient. You know about all the drugs he takes to keep his body from rejecting the heart. Does a number on the rest of him."

Sam fiddled with the now familiar crutches. "What does the doctor say?"

Unable to conceal his worry, Bret's expression was bleak. "They put Dad on the transplant list, but his chances of getting one aren't great. He's not a very good risk and they don't want to waste a viable organ on someone who might not make it."

"Oh, Bret!" Feeling the weight of his pain, she clutched his arm.

"Janie and I both offered to see if we might be a match. Dad refused. Said Janie might need to donate a kidney to one of her children at some point. That she couldn't take the risk. Even though I don't have kids, he said the same thing applied."

Samantha tightened her grip, wishing she could say something, anything that would help.

"You know how he says I'm the one who held things together?" Bret continued. "Not true. He's my rock."

"You've always told me that the Lord looks out for us. Bret, you can't stop believing that now."

"I'm not. It was a fluke when Dad got his new heart. Well, the doctors called it a fluke. We knew it was an answer to prayer." Bret sighed. "But I have to be realistic. Transplant recipients don't have a real long life expectancy. Especially when their kidneys fail."

Samantha's heart tore, feeling Bret's pain as her own.

"Did you mean that?" he asked after a moment. "About the Lord?"

"I…I…"

"You don't have to answer me, Sam. Just Him." Silent for awhile, he bent down, gathering a small handful of soil, then rubbing it between his fingers. "We've had our share of blessings."

"The crops still coming along?"

"First ones have germinated." He shook his head. "That land's been in the family for years. Belonged to my grandparents. I was holding it back for a last-ditch effort—to sell if we had to. Now, it might make us more than it's worth." Bret stood, facing her. "The family considers you a lifesaver."

She held her breath. "And you?"

He reached for her hand, the air between them thick with anticipation. "Haven't you guessed by now?"

"Sam!"

Bret glanced across the park, then cleared his throat. "Looks like Rachel's hunting you down."

Her heart splintered, not wanting to let him go.

"Sam?" he questioned, his voice still husky.

Trying to rein in her feelings physically hurt. "Yes…Rachel. It's probably about therapy." She tried to think. "I might have a session today."

He pulled away and she wondered if he was re-thinking what he'd been about to say. The mixed signals, going hot and cold…both were as confusing as ever.

"The way you're getting around, doesn't look like you'll need therapy much longer."

She didn't want to chit-chat. She wanted to know how he felt.

Bret tapped her crutches. "You've come awfully far."

Samantha found the courage to meet his eyes. "You were sure this day would come. So sure you made me believe it, too."

"You'd have found it out yourself."

She didn't let him shrug off the words. "No. I don't believe I would have."

His brown eyes darkened. "You're something, Samantha Shaw." The breeze picked up her hair, blowing it across her cheek. He reached out and tucked it gently behind one ear. "Really something."

Bret wandered through his parents' backyard, pausing at the door to the greenhouse. Lately, Robert spent a lot of hours working on his orchids. Bret hated the nagging feeling that his dad was nurturing the orchids, tending them so they would be a perfect legacy.

Forcing on a cheerful expression, he entered the warm, humid building. Robert was at the far end of the room, bent over a table. He had lost weight. Not all at once, but day by day, week by week. They had all seen it. Despite dinners of his favorites meant to entice his appetite, he ate little. His clothes hung loosely, while his skin clung to nearly visible bone.

And it was killing Bret to see him this way. "Hey, Dad."

Robert looked up, a glimmer of pleasure in his eyes. "Son."

"Thought you might like to go get some lunch." He wiggled his eyebrows. "Barbecue at Smitty's."

"I think your mother's making something."

"Just chicken salad." *Come on, Dad. You've got to try.*

Robert shrugged half-heartedly. "I'm not all that hungry anyway."

Bret withheld his disappointment. "What are you working on?"

"The impossible. Trying to cross-pollinate these two beauties."

Lifting his chin, Bret nodded. "Makes me think of something you told me about Samantha."

"Oh?"

"That she managed to discover a new species even though it was close to impossible. You've always bucked the odds."

Robert's gaze was steady. "I'm trying my hardest, son."

With two bum kidneys.

"How about you?" Robert continued. "Are you trying with Sam?"

"I'm not sure what—"

"If you don't ask, you'll never know whether you could have a future with her. That's not something you want to look back on with regret. Marrying your mother was the smartest thing I ever did."

"Mom never broke your engagement."

"Sam's not the same person she was eight years ago."

Bret wanted to believe his father was right. Just as he wanted to believe his father would survive. But neither was in his control.

Samantha leaned on her new cane. It had taken her longer than she'd expected, but she had finally graduated from her crutches. Just in time to enjoy the wildflowers. Despite seeing exotic species in foreign locales, none were prettier to her than the native paintbrushes woven amidst fields and fields of bluebonnets.

Strolling around her yard, she checked on the azalea bushes that were now in season. From a delicate light-pink to the deepest fuchsia, the lush blooms were an explosion of color in flower beds all over town.

Pleased by the condition of her own flowers, she walked down the street. Maddie, busy raking, waved from the side yard. Grinning, Sam lifted her cane so Maddie could see. Maddie raised two arms in a victory wave.

At the corner, she turned, walking in the direction of the park. Very few cars passed her. Just a normal day. Kids in school, people at work. A few dogs barked. Ones that were confined behind wooden fences obligingly stuck their muzzles through the slats to be petted.

Samantha heard the sound of a car behind her. It rolled to a stop and Bret stuck his head out. "You training for a marathon?"

Sam laughed. "Thought I'd check on our tree."

"Me, too." Leaving the car idling, he stepped out to open the door for her. "How were you planning to get home?"

She held up a small sack. "Peanut butter and jelly. Thought I'd take a break before I walked back."

"Why don't we pick up some bratwurst rolls, take them to the park?"

Her mouth salivated. "Oh, that does sound good." The Sausage Shack had been in the same family for generations.

Bret made a quick detour to pick up the food, then veered back to the park. "Want to check on the tree first?"

"And let this feast get cold?" She shuddered in mock horror. "I say we grab a bench."

Once settled, they dug past layers of paper, revealing homemade rolls filled with fat, grilled sausages. Grilled sauerkraut gave them their unique taste, along with a sauce that was a highly-guarded family secret.

After a few bites, Sam sighed in utter bliss. "I'd forgotten how incredible these are."

Bret fished for straws and stuck them in soft drink cups, handing her one. "I'd challenge you to find anything this good in a big city."

She laughed softly. "Amazing how much there is right here in our little town. Used to think I had to travel a long way to find what I needed."

"Used to?" His eyes searched hers.

Sam pulled her gaze away, afraid to once again

read too much into his expression. "I've missed this. Being outside, I mean. I used to think of it…" She shrugged. "Just in terms of career. But it's part of me, the outdoors, how I stay grounded. All that time when I had to be inside, I felt as though I was losing myself. I need the connection…to what's real." She laughed self-consciously, then lifted her cane. "Literally being under my own power…. I guess it's making me all gooey. But I think you know what I mean."

He watched her intently. "Yeah. I do."

She fiddled with her cup, then reached for her sandwich. "Don't let yours get cold."

Bret glanced down at his forgotten lunch. "Right."

Some of the birds that had migrated to Mexico had returned along with spring, and they fluttered among the tree branches, checking out any changes to their habitats. Squirrels fussed at birds and people alike as they raced across the grass.

Samantha giggled suddenly. "When Andy and I were little, we named the squirrels in our yard. We'd been watching reruns of *The Beverly Hillbillies* so there was Jed, Granny, Jethro and Elly Mae. Drove our parents batty."

"Sounds like fun."

She realized it had been. And that it didn't hurt to remember the fun times. "Andy would be pleased that we're helping the magnolia."

Bret checked his watch. "Jiminy. Forgot all about the tree. And I have a doctor's appointment at two o'clock."

Worried, she stared at him. "What's wrong?"

"Nothing." He smiled, his eyes clear. "Really. Just a physical, normal tests."

Relieved, Samantha finished her sandwich almost as quickly as he did.

Ditching the papers in a trash barrel, they approached the magnolia. "I really thought we'd lose this old guy." Bret walked to one side of the tall tree. "You've done amazing work."

"I can't take all the credit. Mac, Rachel…and luckily my friend Leonard was willing to give us his advice. He had the all the university's resources to call on. I haven't been using my computer, even to e-mail, since…well, since my accident. So my research time was limited to borrowing Rachel's laptop."

"Still hard for me to believe Peter would go so far." Bret shook his head. "Poor old Mac thinks it's his fault that he didn't notice sooner."

"Well, it's not," she replied staunchly. "Poor guy's done everything he can."

Bret studied her face. "I didn't realize you talked to Mac that much."

"Mostly when I work on the tree. Rachel's been driving me here nearly every day so I run into him a lot. He cares so much about the park. Honestly, I think he feels as though the tree's an ailing child."

"He's an old bachelor." Bret stuck his hands in the pockets of his jeans. "Guess the park is his family."

Sam wondered at the introspective tone in Bret's voice.

Bret pulled out one hand, glancing again at his

watch. "I want to stop by and check on Dad before my appointment."

Sobered, she turned worried eyes toward him. "How is he?"

"He *says* he's all right." Bret put on his sunglasses. "You ready?"

"Sure."

A block from her house, Bret's cell phone rang. He answered it swiftly. "No problem. I can come by later. You sure you don't need help? Okay."

Samantha hated to pry, but she also hated the deepening worry in Bret's expression. "Anything wrong?"

"Mom's taking Dad to the doctor. Says it's his routine tests."

"You don't think so?"

"I don't know anymore." He pulled into her driveway.

"Since you have a few extra minutes, how about a cup of coffee?" Samantha hated to leave him alone with clearly dire thoughts.

Slowly, he turned the key, shutting down the car. "You know you can't make a decent cup of coffee."

She ached for him, knowing what the effort at humor must be costing him. "Which is why I need you to make a fresh pot."

Samantha was glad she'd left the living room drapes open so that the spring sunshine poured inside. Tabby ran to weave between her feet, then deigned to greet Bret.

"You're lucky, you know. Tabby's very picky about who she chooses to play with."

His attempt at smiling was little more than an upturned thinning of his lips. "Yes, lucky."

Instantly she was horrified. "Oh, Bret! I didn't mean—"

"Of course you didn't. So, let's get that coffee going." He made his way to the kitchen.

Trailing after him, Sam wished there was something hopeful she could say or do.

Filling the glass carafe with water, Bret looked out the new, larger window into the backyard. "That mimosa needs to be pruned."

"I'm thinking of planting milkweed. To attract butterflies—monarchs, actually."

"You'll have to plant tons of it. Think your parents will want to keep it up?"

It was her own plan, one she had yet to share with anyone. One that meant she might stay in Rosewood.

Bret measured out some coffee, added it to the machine and clicked it on. "This won't take long."

Sam remembered the cookies Ethel Carruthers had brought over. "I have your favorite cookies…"

"Peanut butter," they finished together.

So much they had shared, so much they still knew about each other. Sam felt her love for Bret stirring, building. It had never died. Hibernated perhaps, but always within reach. For that vague time in the future when she would suddenly realize she wanted it again. Such a fool she'd been.

Mouth dry, she stood without moving, barely breathing.

Somewhere in the muted background, the coffee machine beeped, signaling it was done, the aroma of fresh brew wafting through the kitchen.

Bret took a step closer, reaching out to cradle her cheek.

Eyes closing, she leaned her face into his touch. Wanting, praying for him to realize how much she still loved him.

"Samantha…." His voice, husky and low, was filled with both wonder and promise.

The front doorbell rang stridently, the bell in the hall seeming to clang directly over them.

Sam shook her head, wanting to ignore whoever it was.

The bell rang again, a persistent, steady pealing.

Regret clouding his face, Bret reluctantly stepped back. "It could be someone in my family looking for me…because of Dad."

"Oh." She gathered her wits. "Of course."

Bret reached the door first.

A delivery man from an overnight express service handed him an envelope. "I'll need a signature." He offered a clipboard and pen.

Bret looked over the envelope. "It's not for me. Do you want Ms. Shaw to sign?"

"Not necessary. Not a restricted signature."

After scribbling his name, Bret handed back the clipboard.

"Is it from my parents?" Sam questioned, wondering who in the world was sending her an express package.

"No." He gave her the envelope.

She ripped it open and the papers tumbled out before she could catch them. Bret bent down to pick them up, his gaze skipping over the top one.

His expression hardened before he handed the bundle to her.

"What is it?"

"I was thinking about the future today." He laughed, a brittle sound. "Apparently you were, too."

Uncomprehending, she glanced down at the paper. The reference line jumped out at her: "Offer of Employment." Immediately, she checked the heading. The university. Her friend Leonard. "This is from the university where—"

"I can see that. When were you going to tell me?"

"But it's about…" She shook her head, trying to spit out the jumbled explanation. "Not what you think. I contacted them because—"

"Spare me." Sadness warred with disappointment in his eyes. "I can't believe I was sucked in again. I should have known."

"But—"

The front door still stood open and it took Bret only seconds to disappear through it.

Clutching the papers, Samantha vowed she would get him to understand. She'd lost him once. She wasn't going to again.

Chapter Twenty

Bret's cell phone rang. Seeing that it was Sam's number, he let the call go to voice mail. He was surprised at her persistence. Once she moved back east, he would just be another memory. Again.

He was still kicking himself for believing it could be any other way. He'd heard, via the town grapevine, that Sam's job offer was from a prestigious university.

Bret knew she wouldn't need her full mobility to lecture. But she'd be back in the midst of her elevated circle.

The phone rang again and he muttered under his breath. Irritated, he pulled out his cell, expecting to see Sam's number again. Instead, his heart nearly stopped. It was his parents' home phone number, with 911 tacked on the end. Their emergency code.

Running to his Blazer, he jabbed a number on his speed dial. His mother picked up on the second ring.

"The paramedics are here," she explained in a rush. "Your dad collapsed."

"I can be there in five minutes."

"Just meet us at the hospital." Her voice was shaky. "I'll ride in the ambulance."

Bret beat them to the hospital, flinging his Blazer into a parking spot and running inside to Emergency. As soon as the paramedics arrived with the stretcher, Bret ran to his father's side.

His mother's face was pale and he could see she was fighting tears.

Bret gripped his father's hand. "You trying to scare us, Dad?"

"Too much fuss," he replied in a weak voice.

"Sir, we need you to step aside," one of the paramedics directed.

"We'll be right here, Dad." Swallowing a knot of emotion, Bret watched until the doors swung shut behind the paramedics.

His mother's head was bent as she gave into her sobs. "He was lying there so still. I thought…I thought…."

"It's okay, Mom." The pain in his chest intensified as he held on to his control. "Did you reach Janie?"

"No. You called and then we had to go…"

Pulling out his cell phone, he pushed the speed dial number for Janie, then put his arm around his mother's shoulders.

Janie apparently flew to the hospital, running in to meet them within only a few short minutes. "What does Dr. Beak say?" she panted.

"Nothing yet."

Bret, Janie and their mother joined hands, bending their heads to pray. Then they waited.

And waited.

It seemed that days passed before Dr. Beak emerged. His face was grim.

Nancy stood, one hand pressed tightly to her chest.

"It's not good." Dr. Beak's eyes were filled with compassion. "His only chance is a transplant and he's nowhere near the top of the list."

Bret had never gone against his father's wishes. But he'd prayed for an answer. "I want to be tested to see if I'm a match."

Janie stepped forward. "Me, too."

"No, Dad's right." Bret's voice remained firm, unyielding. "You have kids. One of them might need a transplant someday."

"But—"

Bret cut off his sister. "Janie, I've had all the other tests to be a donor, except for the match. Doctor, can we do the test right away?"

"If you're sure, Bret. My understanding is that your father still doesn't want a family donor."

"That's why I asked you for only the donor qualification tests and not the match. But now, there's not another choice."

Nancy gripped his arm. "Son…"

"I need to go with the doctor, Mom. We'll talk after."

The Lord's reply still resonated in his heart. If there was any chance his father could be saved, Bret should take it.

Samantha cradled her cell phone between her ear and shoulder as she walked into the living room carrying a mug of fresh coffee. She needed the other hand to hang on to her cane.

"A fundraiser for the school? That sounds great, Mom."

"You will have the best time!" Joyce's voice vibrated with excitement. "The kids' parents are cooking all kinds of delicious native foods. And we can't wait for you to actually see what we're doing over here."

"Mom, I'd love to see the school. It's just not the best time."

"Would there be a problem with the flight and your injury? Is it too many hours to sit?"

"Well, no."

"What do you have going on that's so important?"

"Just stuff," Samantha hedged. "That I have to do in Rosewood."

"What's this?" Her mother questioned. "Our hop-on-a-jet girl wants to stay put?"

Sam tried to think of something her mother would accept.

"I can hear you thinking," Joyce commented in a wry tone.

Sighing, Samantha knew she'd been caught out. "I

just don't want to go anywhere right now, Mom. I can't really explain, but I need to be here. In Rosewood."

There was a moment of silence. "You do what you need to, honey. I hope it works out."

Sam had the distinct feeling her mother knew exactly the reason.

"We love you, honey."

"Me, too."

"Do you want to talk to your dad?"

"Sure."

"Here he is."

The front door burst open and Rachel practically flew inside. "Why aren't you answering your phone?"

Sam held it up. "I'm talking with my parents. I saw you beep in. I was going to call you back…" Seeing the grim paleness of Rachel's face, she paused.

Rachel reached for the phone. "Aunt Joyce? Uncle Ed? Sam will call you back later, okay? I need her right now. Thanks. Bye."

"What is it?"

"Bret."

Sam dropped the mug, hot coffee splattering across the wooden floor.

At nearly the same instant she heard a knock on the door.

"Sam?" Maddie poked her head in, taking in the mess, the looks on their faces. "So you know?"

"Not yet!" Sam thought she was practically screaming. Instead the words were a mere croak.

"I just got here," Rachel explained. "Sam, Bret's

giving his dad a kidney. It's Robert's only chance. Life Flight's taking them to Houston so a specialist transplant team can operate."

Sam's mind whirled. "I thought Robert didn't…. Is Bret a match?"

Rachel nodded. "They did the test after Robert's episode."

"Episode?"

"That's what I was told."

"Me, too," Maddie confirmed. "I think he passed out at home and then the ambulance took him to the hospital."

Still crushed under a swirl of confusion, Sam stared at them. "How do you both know this?"

"Church prayer roll. It's a chain. Everyone calls at least three or four other people. In an emergency like this, it works really fast," Maddie explained.

"Oh." Sam tried to process the enormity of the information. "Did you say Houston?"

Rachel nodded.

"What about Nancy and Janie?"

"One of the men at church, Flynn Mallory, owns his own plane. He's flying them."

"How dangerous is the operation?"

Maddie and Rachel looked at each other without speaking.

"I need to get there." Sam looked at her cousin. "I have to."

Rachel didn't argue. "It'll take several hours to drive."

Samantha grabbed her purse.

"Do you want to pack, or—"

"All I need is to get there. To be there when he wakes up."

Even though Samantha and Rachel had occasionally visited Houston, neither was familiar with the sprawling international city. The world-renowned medical center contained mile after impressive mile of hospital complexes. Sam took it as a good sign that the hospital chosen for the transplant was St. Luke's.

It took some tricky navigating, but they finally found the right building and parked. Sam had barely spoken during the trip, digging her nails into the upholstery until her fingers were numb.

Although stiff from the ride, she hurried out of the car, walking with Rachel through the huge parking structure. "What if Nancy and Janie don't want us here? Bret's really angry with me. He may have told them."

"You love Bret, don't you?" Rachel halted, turning to stare at her. "Don't you?"

"Yes."

"That's all that matters."

By the time they traveled the long corridors that eventually led them to surgery, Samantha was leaning heavily on her cane. But nothing was going to stop her. Seeing Bret's family did make her pause. Herb had apparently ridden along and he sat with Janie, holding her hand. Trying to be inconspicuous, Sam sidled to one side. But with her cane, she wasn't as inconspicuous as she'd hoped. Nancy looked up and saw her.

Still uncertain, Samantha froze.

Nancy jumped up, rushing over, enveloping Samantha in a huge hug. "I'm so glad you're here."

"I…I just had to come. To see…to see how Bret…."

"I know."

"They wouldn't tell us anything downstairs. Privacy laws and we're not family, and…"

Nancy nodded. "They spent a while making sure Robert's stable. Even though Dr. Beak did all the tests they need to have on Bret, they still took more blood here. Something about a cross-match." Nancy clasped and unclasped her hands, her red-rimmed eyes anxious.

Janie and Herb joined them. "They need to begin the operation as soon as possible for Dad," Janie explained. "But everything has to be right."

"This is a wonderful hospital," Rachel said quietly.

"That's what I've been telling Janie," Herb agreed. "Dr. Beak did his residency here. Apparently that's why he was able to get the surgery scheduled so quickly. And they accepted his evaluation—the tests he ran on Bret. Luckily, he'd seen Robert for his regular tests this week, so…."

Silence fell over the small group like a pallor.

"Have you met the doctor?" Samantha questioned, wishing they knew more. Wishing they knew *anything*.

"Doctors. Plural," Janie explained. "It's a whole transplant team. Well, actually two. One team for Dad, one for Bret. The doctors should be good. The coordinator said they've performed over twelve hundred kidney transplants in the last twenty years here at St. Luke's. And with Dad already having the heart transplant…." Her voice wobbled.

Samantha closed her eyes, unable to imagine how the family would cope without its patriarch. No more than she could imagine herself without Bret, she realized, the restriction in her chest painful and choking. What if something went wrong with the surgery? People assumed that the donor's part of the process was safe, but it wasn't guaranteed.

Nothing was guaranteed. All they had to count on was their faith. The realization had been growing like an untended seedling, sprouting despite its lack of care. A silent prayer bubbled inside her, for Robert and Bret. Even if Bret never looked her way again…. All that mattered was his safety.

Herb led Janie back to their chairs. Nancy stood alone, looking lost. Bret had always been her stalwart during these times, the one who had held the family together. Samantha swallowed, remembering how she'd dismissed this part of his life so long ago, thinking her career was just as important.

Stepping forward, Samantha slipped her arm under Nancy's. The older woman lifted her gaze. "It's hard. Waiting for our men."

Samantha swallowed.

Rachel waved in the direction of the vending machines and left.

"I think she's gone for coffee," Samantha murmured. "Would you like to sit down?"

"Yes, I think so." Nancy settled in one of the chairs and Sam sat next to her. "They gave us a book to read on the transplant process. I...couldn't make myself read it, but if you..."

"That's all right. I'm not good with all that technical stuff."

Nancy smiled faintly. "Bret always took care of that before. During Robert's heart surgeries. Helps that he knows Latin." She glanced over at Sam. "Of course. You know Latin as well."

"In the horticultural sense. Bret's always been better at languages. I remember how he picked up Spanish like it was nothing. And..." Memories washed over her, forming a knot in her throat.

Nancy patted her hand. Samantha noticed that she wore what must be Robert's wedding ring on her middle finger. Of course. He couldn't have it on in surgery. It was a solid-looking band, one that was loose even on Nancy's largest finger. When Nancy withdrew her hand, she clutched on to the ring like a lifeline.

Robert and Nancy had been married as long as Sam's parents. Eyes downcast, Samantha wondered how it would be to know that your love was forever. She'd always taken her parents' marriage for granted, not realizing how special it was to find that one person in the entire world who was meant only for you.

No one spoke as they waited. Time crawled more

slowly than sea turtles laboriously heading back into the ocean. Rachel was gone for an unusually long time. When she returned, she carried three small lap blankets, which she'd bought in the gift shop.

"Gets chilly just waiting," Rachel explained, handing one to each of the women. For Herb she'd brought a sports magazine.

"Oh, Rach," Samantha murmured, grateful that her cousin was not only her best friend, but also as close as a sister.

"I needed something to do. And I'm guessing we're going to drown in coffee before the operation's over."

"Cocoa," Sam suggested. "It's more comforting than coffee."

Rachel smiled. "Good idea."

Samantha started to rise but Rachel waved her back down. "Remember, I need to stay busy."

"She's a sweet girl," Nancy remarked. "Can certainly tell you're related."

Samantha bit down on her lower lip. "That's kind of you to say. I haven't exactly been the sort of person to endear myself. The way I treated Bret." Her voice broke. "I wish…"

"You were young and full of dreams. Bret understood that."

Samantha shook her head. "He was hurt and angry."

"He was young, too. You were in different places in your lives."

Tears swimming in her eyes, Sam tilted her face toward the ceiling. "I ruined everything. Forever."

"I know something about long relationships. How they strain, and bend, and strengthen." Nancy took her hand. "Where there's love, there's always hope."

Stricken, Sam dashed away her tears. "I'm so sorry! Thinking about myself when you're worried about both your husband and son."

"That doesn't change. But it helps to have someone to lean on. Bret will need that."

"Bret? But he's always so strong." Strong for his mother, his sister. The rock…

"You know how Dad says I'm the one who held things together? Not true. He's my rock." Bret's words reverberated in her thoughts.

Him need her? Could it be possible?

Bret's throat felt dry. And scratchy. Like he'd been chewing sand. But there was a soft, warm touch on his forehead, then fingers gently combing his hair back. Nice. But it was so white. Blindingly white.

Memory returned like a suddenly lit match and he forced his eyes open. "Dad?"

Although the word was as faint and scratchy as his throat, the soft touch stopped. "He's in recovery, doing well."

His eyes focused. "Sam?"

"Your mother and Janie are waiting to see your father. They peeked in to see how you're doing. The doctor says you came through with flying colors."

"Dad..." He swallowed, afraid to ask. "Any complications?"

"None." Her smile was tremulous. "It's a miracle."

Miracle? The anesthesia must not have worn away. Sam didn't believe in miracles. "What are you doing here?"

She bit down on her lip, looking more nervous than he could ever recall. "Making sure you're all right." He tried to clear his throat and she immediately turned to the bedside table. "The doctor said you can have ice chips." She dipped into a cup, then fed him a little ice.

He watched her as it melted.

Still nervous, she put the spoon back in the cup. "You can only have a few at a time."

"You drove all the way to Houston?"

"Technically, Rachel drove."

He blinked. "Has the anesthesia worn off?"

"Not completely, I guess. They said you'd be drowsy. Why?"

"Aren't you supposed to be headed back east? To take that fancy new job?"

She kept her eyes downcast, digging in the cup. "Don't be silly. I've got a magnolia tree to nurse."

Was it possible? Ignoring all the tubes and wires attached to his arm, he grasped her hand. "Samantha?"

Eyelids opened slowly, revealing deep-blue jewels of longing. And was that love?

"Is that all you have to nurse?"

Her lips trembled.

"What about a man with only one kidney, but a heart consumed with love?"

Tears sparkled as they spilled over long lashes. "I think I can handle that."

He pulled her closer, touching her cheek, making sure she was real. "If this is a dream, I hope it never ends."

"It's a dream," she agreed. "But we get to share it together."

Epilogue

"To think we ever worried that this old place wouldn't make it." Robert shook his head, his eyes twinkling as he looked around the well-stocked nursery. With Robert back at his fighting weight, his complexion was a ruddy pink, a visible sign of his good health. It had been a long battle, weeks in the hospital, months to completely recover, but he'd done it.

He told everyone that Nancy nagged him back to health. Said he had to get well or she would have driven him crazy. Considering the pair still walked hand in hand, people winked as they listened to his version of the story.

"With Bret in charge?" Nancy tsked at her husband. "Never had a doubt. Our son has quite a head on his shoulders. You ought to know that better than anyone."

Robert had come to terms with Bret's decision to donate his kidney. It was difficult, even for the head of the family, to argue with an answer to prayer. And it definitely had been.

Bret's recovery had been swift, complication-free. Despite all the dire warnings of what could happen to either Robert or Bret, both had fared well. Blessed. Samantha thought it. Believed it. Robert, Bret and most certainly herself. They were deluged in blessings.

"Sustainable food crops." Robert shook his head. "I would never have thought of something like that. But you two…"

Sam smiled at her soon to be father-in-law. "Bret's done all the work. I just had the idea."

"Just?" He grinned.

Nancy held up some of the wedding phlox grown at the nursery. "Sam? What do you think of these as some of the flowers for the ceremony?"

Although Samantha had spent her life living and learning plants, she wasn't picky about the flowers. Or any of the other wedding details. All she could focus on was the groom. "Fine."

Nancy's smile was rueful. "I know you said I could pick what I want to arrange, but it's *your* wedding. And you're the plant expert."

Sam smiled, something that came easily now. "I trust your judgment. Between Aunt Trudy, Rachel and Maddie, I have so much wedding advice it's sort of become a haze."

An understanding look filled Nancy's eyes. "If you're sure…"

"Very." She glanced at her watch. "Yipes. I told

Bret I'd meet him at four at my house." Sam raised her voice. "Herb, I need to take off. You okay for a while?"

He waved her on. "Get going." Herb now managed the shop since Bret spent so much time cultivating the food crops. Sam divided her time between the shop and helping with the cultivation. They'd had to hire another employee to tend to the native species, bedding plants and Christmas trees. Although the business wasn't booming yet, it was reviving, and even better, growing.

Now able to walk proficiently with just her cane, Sam could drive as well. Freedom. She had it on all levels. Physically, emotionally, spiritually. Blinking back tears of gratitude, she headed to her house. Bret's Blazer was parked in the driveway.

Excited to see him, she practically jumped from the car, balancing easily on her cane. There wouldn't be any more trudging through forests and jungles, but the only place she wanted to be was home. In Rosewood. With Bret.

He waved just then, from the living room window. So instead of entering through the back as she usually did, Sam headed up the steps and threw open the front door.

"Surprise!" Sam's parents rushed toward her, arms outstretched.

Her own feet reacted only moments later and they met somewhere in the middle. "Mom, Dad!"

A dozen hugs and exclamations later, Sam beamed at them. "I don't understand. You weren't supposed to be here until a few days before the wedding!"

Ed and Joyce looked first at each other and then at their daughter.

"We're home," Ed told her.

"For good," Joyce added.

Sam stared at them in shocked disbelief. "You're not going back?"

Ed shook his head. "The school's on strong footing and the funding is permanently in place."

"So we turned the management over to locals. It's their school, after all," Joyce said with pride.

"And you won't miss it?" Sam questioned, afraid to believe it could be true, that her whole family was home, together.

"We'll always care about the kids…" Ed began.

"But we're ready to be home with our own child," Joyce finished for him. "To return to Rosewood."

Realizing Bret hadn't said a word, Sam turned to him. "Did you know about this?"

He grinned. "Afraid so."

"And you didn't say a word…" She'd been fretting the last several weeks, worried that her parents' flight might be delayed, that they'd miss the service. "That couldn't have been easy."

Bret looked at her with love. "Worth every minute."

"Without him, we couldn't have pulled it off," Ed explained. "We'd made the decision, but timing the surprise was tricky."

Sam leaned her head on Bret's shoulder as he clasped her waist, pulling her close. "Everything's… so perfect. So blessed."

* * *

Breathtaking Casa Blanca lilies with their dramatic blossoms, showy carolina wedding phlox, heirloom roses and elegant calla lilies in varying hues of white—so many flowers filled the church that it smelled like spring. New beginnings. New promises.

Afternoon sunshine streamed through the exquisite stained-glass windows; prisms of refracted color spilled through the sanctuary filled with friends, family, half of Rosewood.

Standing in the vestibule, Samantha peeked inside, then caught her breath at the beautiful arrangement of flowers, candles and classic satin draping. She couldn't have envisioned anything more beautiful.

Joyce tugged the bottom of Sam's full skirt, making certain it was positioned just right. The exquisite silk and lace confection was a dream. The fitted bodice showcased her hourglass-shaped figure, then flowed into a skirt so full it couldn't trip her up. "Sweetheart, I'd better go take my seat."

Sam turned, meeting her mother's loving gaze. "Thank you. For everything. Especially coming back."

Joyce blinked back a tear. "It's been our dream… our family together again."

"Aunt Joyce, you're going to make her start blubbing again and then I'll have to redo her makeup." Rachel fussed with the train on Sam's dress.

Joyce hugged Sam, then patted Rachel's arm. "I've missed you."

Rachel winked, then turned back to Sam. "Wow. I

thought I'd be jumping up and down. Instead, I feel as weepy as your mom."

"Not you, too!"

"Stupid, huh?" As maid of honor, Rachel was dressed in a simple but stunning champagne silk. "Just that now you'll be Bret's."

"And you'll still be my best friend and sister." Sam swallowed, fighting the tears.

"Rats. We'll both wreck our makeup. Take a deep breath." Rachel demonstrated. "No crying. At least not until after the ceremony."

"Right." Sam pressed her cousin's hand. "Is Maddie ready?"

Rachel nodded, swiping at the one tear that had crept past her best defenses. "She looks great. And, yes, Lillian's sitting with her friends and she's fine."

Samantha saw her father waiting for her. "Looks like we're ready."

Grabbing her solitary calla lily, Rachel straightened her shoulders. "That means I'm up." She darted one last look. "Love you, cuz."

Not waiting for Sam's reply, Rachel took her place, then started gliding up the aisle to the beckoning organ music.

Maddie was next. She smiled brightly at Samantha, then walked forward.

Taking her arm, Sam's father tucked it under his elbow. "You look beautiful, punkin."

The childhood nickname nearly did her in. "Oh, Dad."

"We're so proud of you." He patted her hand. "I

have orders from your mother not to make you cry, but you know how I feel."

Sam's throat clogged with emotion. "Me, too." She picked up her bouquet of exquisite orchids that Robert and Nancy had made for her.

Rachel and Maddie stood at the altar watching. But Samantha's eyes immediately sought out Bret. Flanked on one side by best man Matt Whitaker and groomsman J.C., he waited, his gaze intense.

Music from the organ grew louder as strains of the wedding march began, then swelled to fill the chapel.

Holding tight to her father so she wouldn't stumble without her cane, Sam walked up the aisle, aware of the smiles and support surrounding her, but having eyes only for her groom.

Bret's gaze burned as it remained solely on her.

The music dimmed and the traditional ceremony progressed. The pastor began the service, but Sam barely heard the words. Not until her father squeezed her arm.

"Who gives this woman to be married?"

"Her mother and I." Then her father carefully placed Sam's hand in Bret's.

Age-old vows came alive in the lovely chapel, stirring all who watched, all who listened.

"In sickness and in health…" A test they'd already passed.

"For richer or poorer…" Having each other was all the wealth they needed.

Words and music seemed to dim around them both

until the pastor announced: "I now pronounce you husband and wife."

Bret carefully lifted her veil. Their lips met in a tender kiss of promise.

Music escalated, trumpeting the proclamation. Bret and Samantha swept down the aisle and outside to the reception on the church grounds.

Well-wishers crowded around. In the background, a harp, violin and cello played as people spilled out of the church and into the beautiful spring day.

Samantha felt as though she was floating on clouds, ones she hoped never fell to earth. When there was finally a break in the receiving line, she pressed closer to Bret.

"Think it's still a dream?"

He turned to her, his eyes filled with a tenderness that made Sam catch her breath. "Absolutely."

"Everything's so perfect," she murmured. "Today… you, my parents…"

Smiling, Bret caught her hand. "Happy as I am to have them back, I'm sure glad they went to Africa."

Sam lifted her eyebrows.

"Think I could have talked you into walking down the aisle if I hadn't pulled you from that fire?" His brown eyes glinted, the old teasing light back permanently.

Overflowing with happiness, Sam grinned. "By the time you tell our children this tale, you really will have climbed to the top of a rickety ten-story building to rescue me."

"I want about a dozen, that look just like you."

She shuddered. "Uh-uh. Like *you*."

Bret hooked his arm around her waist, tugging her a fraction closer. "I don't know." A light breeze carried the scents of newly blooming spring. It also tousled Samantha's hair, tufting dark strands against pale, creamy skin. "The most beautiful woman in Rosewood, and you're mine."

She leaned in as he covered her lips with his.

He cupped the back of her head, searching the depths of her eyes. "Do you suppose we really are still dreaming?"

Slowly, enticingly, her mouth curved upward. "I hope so. Because this is the dream where we meet again, fall back in love and live happily ever after."

"Promise?"

Tracing the outline of his jaw, she paused, love shining so brightly in her eyes it nearly overshadowed her beauty. "You are my heart, my life, my forever."

His arms encircled her, holding her so close, even the barest gasp of breath couldn't pass between them. "Forever."

* * * * *

Dear Reader,

The seasons of our lives often parallel the unfolding of nature—including the bright promise of spring. For those with little hope, spring often seems as though it will never arrive.

In telling Samantha's story, I am reminded of special people in my life with special needs. And the promise of hope that sustains us.

I am also reminded of dreams long put aside that are stirred and brought to life. And of the remarkable people who allow us to pursue those dreams. Spouses who support us, children who wait patiently and friends who believe in us when we don't believe in ourselves.

For all of these incredible people in our lives, I have returned to Rosewood, a place where hope flourishes, love binds, and the promise of spring always blossoms. Blessings,

Bonnie K. Winn

QUESTIONS FOR DISCUSSION

1. Is it possible to rekindle a relationship after years apart? Why or why not?

2. Which do you feel was the bigger issue between Samantha and Bret: Samantha's disability or the importance of family?

3. Trust is vital to a good relationship. Once it's broken, it is difficult to repair. Do you agree or disagree?

4. Did you agree with Bret's initial decision to stay in Rosewood rather than marry Samantha and leave his family? What would you have done in his place?

5. Do you think they would have been happy if Samantha had stayed in Rosewood eight years ago and married Bret rather than pursuing her career goals?

6. Dealing with problem employees isn't easy. Should Bret have fired Peter rather than putting him on probation?

7. Are family businesses a thing of the past? Or have we learned from the recession that bigger is not better? Do you prefer shopping at mom-and-pop stores or large chains? Discuss why.

8. It took quite some time for Bret to forgive Samantha. In his place, would you have acted differently?

9. Do you believe we can return home after a long absence and be happy? Have you ever done so? How did it turn out?

10. A sense of community is important in Rosewood. Is this something that still exists where you live? Describe.

11. Did you understand Samantha's reasoning for not wanting to tell her parents she had returned? How would you have handled the situation?

Love Inspired®
SUSPENSE
RIVETING INSPIRATIONAL ROMANCE

Watch for our new series of
edge-of-your-seat suspense novels.
These contemporary tales
of intrigue and romance
feature Christian characters
facing challenges to their faith...
and their lives!

NOW AVAILABLE IN REGULAR & LARGER-PRINT FORMATS

Steeple
Hill®

Visit:
www.SteepleHill.com

LISUSDIR10

Love Inspired
HISTORICAL
INSPIRATIONAL HISTORICAL ROMANCE

Engaging stories of romance,
adventure and faith,
these novels are set in
various historical periods
from biblical times
to World War II.

NOW AVAILABLE!

**Steeple
Hill®**